HARPER'S JUSTICE ORIGINS

ASHES
and
OATHS

R.J. SLOANE

desert life
media

Ashes and Oaths: Harper's Justice Origins
By R.J. Sloane

Publisher:
Desert Life Media, LLC
Gilbert, AZ 85295

www.rjsloanewesterns.com

Printed in the United States of America

ISBN: 978-1-960217-68-4

When justice is executed,
it is a joy to the righteous
but a terror to evildoers.
—Proverbs 21:15 CSB

Prologue - My First Family

———————

MY NAME IS Shane Harper and these are the stories of how I kept my first family alive.

No one taught me how to be a man, a provider, a father, or a warrior. No one made sure I said my prayers at night. That I had a blanket to keep me warm. No one wiped my tears when I was scared. And in those early days, I was scared a lot.

My sister Lilian kept me sane. Sacrificed herself in many ways. We worked together as the oldest two, ensuring the others had a hope—she always believed a prayer—of making it to the other side as decent folk.

I sit here now in a warm house with a full pantry and grandchildren at my feet, and sometimes it feels like those years happened to someone else. But they didn't. They happened to me. To us. To six kids who should've had parents and safety and childhood, but got none of those things.

"Grandpa?" Emma tugs at my sleeve, her eyes wide. "Were you really only thirteen?"

"Thirteen," I confirm. "Lilian was twelve. Justine was ten. Hayley was five. Flynn was four. And Ike wasn't even two years old yet."

"That's younger than me," Jake breathes, and I see him trying to imagine it—being responsible for keeping anyone alive when you're still figuring out how to keep yourself fed.

"It is," I say. "Too young. But life doesn't always care

what's fair or right. Sometimes it just hands you an impossible situation and expects you to figure it out."

My wife Tessa moves quietly around the room, lighting lamps as the winter sun sets outside. She's heard these stories before—most of them, anyway. There are some things I've only ever told her in the dark of our bedroom, when the memories get too heavy to carry alone. But she knows enough. She knows what those years cost me.

"Tell them," she says softly, settling into her chair with her knitting. "They're old enough to understand."

I look at my grandchildren. Clara's eldest girl with her mother's serious eyes. Jude's boy with his father's restless energy. Two more, younger but old enough to listen. They carry the Harper name, and they deserve to know what it meant before it meant rangers and marshals and justice.

"It started on Christmas Eve, 1880," I begin. "I'd been hunting all day in the cold, trying to find something—anything—to feed my siblings. All I'd managed to get was one skinny rabbit."

"One rabbit for six people?" Emma asks.

"One rabbit for six people," I confirm. "And do you know what? We made it work. Because that's what you do when you love people. You make it work."

The fire crackles in the hearth. Outside, the desert wind whispers against the walls of our sturdy house. My grandchildren lean in closer, and I can see them trying to reconcile the grandfather they know—the one with the comfortable home and the easy smile for them—with the desperate boy I'm describing.

"These stories aren't easy ones," I tell them. "They're not about adventure or glory. They're about survival. About the choices you make when there are no good options. About what it costs to protect the people you love."

"We want to hear them," Jake says firmly. He's got his father's determination, that one.

Tessa catches my eye and gives me a small nod. It's alright, that look says. They need to know. And you need to tell it.

So I do.

"One rabbit," I say again. "Six kids. Christmas Eve. Let me tell you about that night..."

1 - One Rabbit

───────────

Christmas Eve, 1880

THE RABBIT HUNG limp from my belt. One rabbit. Six kids. Christmas Eve.

I was thirteen years old, and I'd been the man of the house for three months. Mama had gone on to glory months before that.

The December cold bit through my threadbare coat as I trudged back toward the ranch house. My hands ached from hours of hunting in the grassy valley, fingers stiff around Pa's old rifle. The sun was sinking fast, painting the Arizona sky in shades of orange and gold that would've been beautiful if I had time to notice such things.

I didn't.

My breath came out in white puffs as I walked, each exhale reminding me I was still alive. Still moving. Still responsible for five other lives that depended on me not failing.

Pa had been gone since September. Maybe arrested. Maybe just run off. Either way, he'd left us with a failing ranch, empty cupboards, and debts we couldn't pay. The neighbors had helped at first—brought over food, checked on us—but charity only went so far. Eventually, folks expected you to stand on your own two feet.

Even if you were just a kid.

The house came into view, smoke rising thin from the chimney. At least they'd kept the fire going. That was something. Lilian would've made sure of it. At twelve, she tried her best to mother the younger ones, but she was still just a kid herself. We were both pretending we knew what we were doing.

We didn't.

I pushed open the door, and the smell hit me first. Bread. Somehow, Lilian and Justine had made bread with the last scraps of flour we had. The warmth of the house wrapped around me like a blanket, and for just a moment, I let myself feel the exhaustion in my bones.

"Shane!" Hayley's voice cut through my thoughts. She was five years old with our mama's blond hair and eyes that saw too much. She ran up and wrapped her arms around my waist. "Did you get something?"

I held up the rabbit. "Christmas dinner."

Her face lit up brighter than a struck match in a dark barn. "That's wonderful!"

It wasn't wonderful. It was one small rabbit that would barely feed us all. But I wasn't going to tell her that.

Flynn appeared from the back room, his reddish-brown hair sticking up at odd angles. At four, he already had that restless energy that made him both helpful and exhausting. "Can I help clean it?"

"You're too little for that, buddy."

"Where's Ike?"

"In the bedroom with Justine."

I found our youngest brother in the small bedroom he shared with Flynn—barely two years old, too young to understand why Christmas felt different this year. Justine sat with him, her blond hair falling over her shoulder as she played with him, trying to keep him occupied and warm. At ten, she had Mama's gentle way about her, always trying to smooth things over and make everyone feel better.

I stood and found Lilian in the kitchen, her strawberry-blond hair tied back as she worked. She looked up when I came in, and I saw the question in her eyes before she asked it.

"That's all you got?"

"That's all there was."

She pressed her lips together and nodded. She'd learned not to complain. None of us had that luxury anymore. "I'll make it work. Justine and I made bread, and we've got some beans left. We can stretch it."

"The decorations look nice," I said, gesturing to the pine branches and fabric strips the kids had hung around the room. It wasn't much, but they'd tried.

"Hayley and Flynn worked hard on them." Lilian's voice softened. "They wanted it to feel like Christmas."

I looked around at the sparse room. The patched furniture. The thin curtains. The cracks in the walls we'd stuffed with rags to keep the cold out. This wasn't what Christmas was supposed to look like.

But it was what we had.

"Let me get this rabbit cleaned," I said. "We'll make it work."

Dinner was quiet. We sat around the small table—all six of us squeezed together—and said grace over our meager meal. Lilian had done her best, stretching that rabbit and those beans into something that at least filled our bellies a little. The bread helped, even if it was more air than substance.

Ike barely touched his food. Too young to understand, maybe, but old enough to feel the absence. Hayley ate with determination, like she was trying to convince herself it was a feast. Flynn wolfed his down without seeming to taste it. Justine smiled and made encouraging comments, but I could see the worry in her brown eyes.

And Lilian... Lilian just looked tired.

After dinner, we sat by the fire. Justine had a Bible open on her lap—our mother's Bible, worn at the edges from years of reading. She read the Christmas story aloud, her voice steady and clear.

"And she brought forth her firstborn son, and wrapped him in swaddling clothes, and laid him in a manger; because there was no room for them in the inn."

I stared at the flames and thought about Mary and Joseph, alone in a stable with nothing but each other and a newborn baby. No room. No help. Just faith that somehow, it would be enough.

I wasn't sure I had that kind of faith.

"Can we sing?" Hayley asked when Justine finished reading.

So we sang. Our voices were thin and off-key, but we sang every carol we could remember. *Silent Night*, *Hark the Herald Angels Sing*, and *Joy to the World*. Hayley's small voice got louder with each song, and even Flynn stopped fidgeting long enough to join in. Ike clapped his hands, not understanding the words but caught up in the moment.

For a few minutes, we almost forgot we were six kids alone in the Arizona Territory with nothing but hope and each other.

Almost.

After the younger ones finally fell asleep—Ike curled up with Flynn, Hayley tucked in with Justine—I sat by the dying fire. Lilian joined me, wrapping a thin blanket around her shoulders.

"You did good today, Shane."

I shook my head. "One rabbit isn't good."

"It's more than nothing." She was quiet for a moment. "You're keeping us alive. That's more than Pa ever did."

I didn't answer. What was there to say? She was right. Pa had never cared if we ate or froze or died. He'd cared about his criminal empire, his reputation, his own survival. We'd always been an afterthought.

"Do you think we'll make it?" Lilian's voice was small in the darkness.

I looked at my sister just twelve years old, trying to be strong, trying to hold together a family that was falling apart. I thought about lying to her. Telling her everything would be fine. That someone would come help us.

But I'd never lied to Lilian, and I wasn't about to start.

"I don't know," I said. "But I'm going to make sure we do. Whatever it takes."

She leaned her head against my shoulder. "I know you will."

After she went to bed, I sat alone by the fire. The house was quiet except for the soft breathing of my siblings and the occasional pop from the dying embers. I was exhausted. Bone-tired in a way that had nothing to do with hunting all day and everything to do with carrying weight I was never meant to hold.

I was thirteen years old. I should've been learning to rope cattle and ride horses and maybe even thinking about girls. Instead, I was trying to figure out how to keep five kids alive through winter with no money, no help, and no hope that things would get better.

I stared at the dying fire and made myself a promise.

We would survive this. All of us. I would hunt every day if I had to. Work every job I could find. Steal if it came to that. Whatever it took to keep them fed and warm and alive.

Lilian was twelve. Justine was ten. Hayley was five. Flynn was four. Ike wasn't even two yet.

They were my family. The only thing in this world that mattered.

And I would not let them down.

I didn't pray. I'd stopped believing God listened to people like us a long time ago. But I made that vow to myself— to them—and I meant it with everything in me.

The fire died down to coals, and I finally let myself close my eyes.

Tomorrow I'd wake up and do it all over again. Hunt. Provide. Protect. Survive.

But tonight, on Christmas Eve, we'd had each other.

And somehow, it had been enough.

Interlude - By The Fire

———————

THE FIRE HAS burned lower while I talked. My grand-children are quiet, absorbing what I've told them.

"But you made it," Emma says finally. "You all made it through that winter."

"We did," I confirm. "Barely. There were mornings I woke up not sure if Ike had made it through the night. Times when Flynn was so cold his lips turned blue. But we kept each other warm. We kept each other alive."

"How, Grandpa?" Jake asks. "How did you do it?"

"Strategy," I say. "I had to start thinking ahead, planning, creating systems. I couldn't protect everyone all the time, so I had to be smart about it."

"What kind of systems?"

I smile slightly, remembering. The memory isn't pleasant, but there's satisfaction in knowing it worked. "Well, that brings me to the next story. The one about a red bandanna and a warning system that saved my sisters' lives more times than I can count."

Tessa looks up from her knitting, and I see understanding in her eyes. She knows this story. Knows what it cost me to be that strategic at fourteen.

"Your grandfather learned something important that year," she says quietly. "That being strong isn't always about being the biggest or the toughest. Sometimes it's about being the smartest."

"That's right," I say. "I was fourteen years old, barely tall enough to look most men in the eye. I couldn't fight off grown outlaws. Couldn't stop them from coming to the ranch. But I could outsmart them. And I could protect my sisters in ways they never even knew about."

"How?" Emma leans forward.

"Let me tell you about the summer after that Christmas. About the day I realized I couldn't be everywhere at once—and what I did about it."

The fire crackles in the hearth. Outside, the wind has picked up, rattling the windows. But inside, we're warm and safe, and my grandchildren are listening with a rapt attention that tells me they understand these aren't just stories. This is their family's history. Their legacy.

"It started," I say, "with my sister Lilian walking toward the barn, humming like it was any other day..."

2 - The Red Bandana

————————

June 1881

THE SOUND OF Lilian's humming froze me mid-step.

She was walking toward the barn, laundry basket balanced on her hip, completely unaware that three horses stood tied to the hitching post near the barn door. Three horses that hadn't been there when I'd left to check the fence line an hour ago.

My heart slammed against my ribs. The Mason brothers were inside. I'd recognize those horses anywhere—Victor's black gelding, Caleb's paint, and Bart's roan. They'd ridden in while I was gone, probably using the back trail so I wouldn't see them coming.

And Lilian was heading straight for them.

I dropped the wire cutters and ran, my boots kicking up dust as I crossed the yard. She was maybe thirty feet from the barn door when I caught up to her.

"Lilian." I kept my voice low, steady. Didn't want to spook her into doing something that would draw attention.

She turned, strawberry-blond hair glinting in the harsh Arizona sun. At thirteen, she still had that hopeful look in her eyes sometimes, like she believed things might get better. I hated that I was about to take that away.

"I need you to go back to the house."

Her brow furrowed. "I was just going to hang the—"

"Now." I took the basket from her hip. "Take Justine and Hayley. Make sure they stay inside."

Something in my tone must have gotten through because the hope in her eyes dimmed. She glanced past me toward the barn, and I saw the moment she understood. Her face went pale.

"How long have they been here?"

"Don't know. But they're here now, and you need to be in the house."

She nodded, swallowed hard, and turned back toward the house without another word. I watched until she disappeared through the door, then carried the laundry basket back myself. I hung the damp clothes on the line as quickly as I could manage, keeping my back to the barn but my ears sharp for any sound that meant trouble. Once I pinned the last shirt, I set the empty basket on the porch and headed to the barn.

My hands were shaking. Not from fear—though maybe they should have been—but from the realization that had just hit me like a kick to the gut.

I couldn't protect everyone all the time.

The thought sat in my chest like a stone as I pushed open the barn door. Scar-faced Victor Mason stood in the shadows near the tack room, his black clothes making him look like something that had crawled out of a nightmare. Caleb Mason leaned against a stall, cleaning his fingernails with a knife. Bart Mason was nowhere in sight—probably already in the hidden room behind the padlocked door.

"Whelp." Victor's voice was cold, flat. He looked at me the way a man might look at a stray dog he was deciding whether to kick or ignore.

"Afternoon." I kept my voice neutral, didn't show the fear that crawled up my spine whenever Victor was around. He'd killed men. More than one. Pa had laughed about it once, like it was something to be proud of.

"Your old man around?"

"Out on business."

"When's he back?"

"Didn't say."

Victor studied me for a long moment, and I forced myself to hold his gaze. Fourteen years old and barely tall enough to look him in the eye, but I'd learned early that showing weakness was dangerous.

"We'll wait," he finally said, and turned back to whatever conversation I'd interrupted.

I grabbed a pitchfork and started mucking stalls, working within earshot but not close enough to seem like I was listening. They talked in low voices about routes and timing, about someone named Henderson who was getting nervous and needed handling.

I kept working, kept my head down, and tried not to think about what would have happened if Lilian had walked through that door.

That night, I lay awake in the loft, staring at the rough-hewn beams above my head. Flynn and Ike were asleep nearby, Flynn's arm thrown over his face, Ike curled into a tight ball despite the summer heat. Below, I could hear Lilian moving around, probably checking on the girls one more time before she let herself sleep.

I couldn't stop replaying that moment—Lilian walking toward the barn, humming like it was any other day. Thirty feet. Maybe less. If I'd been five minutes later getting back from the fence line, she would have walked right into that barn.

And then what?

I knew what Caleb Mason wanted from Lilian. I'd seen the way he looked at her, the way he found excuses to corner her when he thought no one was watching. I'd interrupted him twice now, made myself visible at just the right moment to make him back off.

But I couldn't be there every time.

The realization settled over me like a weight. I was one person. Fourteen years old, not big enough to fight off grown men, not strong enough to stand between my sisters and every threat that walked onto this ranch.

I couldn't be everywhere at once.

So I had to be smarter.

I turned onto my side, mind working through the problem like I was planning a hunt. What did I need? A way to warn them when danger was present. A signal they could see from the house, something that would tell them to stay away from the barn without me having to explain why.

Something simple. Something that wouldn't raise questions from Pa or the gang if they noticed it.

The idea came to me just before dawn, and I knew immediately it would work.

Three days later, I found the red bandanna in Pa's room shoved in a drawer with a bunch of other gear he'd left behind. It was faded and worn, but the color was still bright enough to be seen from a distance. I also grabbed a blue one, figuring I'd need an all-clear signal too.

The hat hooks by the barn door had been there since before Ma died, rusty nails driven into the weathered wood. No one ever used them. Perfect.

That afternoon, while the Mason brothers were holed up in their hidden room and Pa was off doing whatever criminal business he did, I tested the system. Hung the red bandanna on the hook and walked back to the house, checking sight lines from different windows.

You could see it clear as day from the kitchen. From the yard. From anywhere the girls might be when they were doing chores.

Now I just had to teach them what it meant.

———

"WHY?" JUSTINE ASKED, her brown eyes serious as she studied the red bandanna hanging on the hook. She was ten, old enough to ask questions, young enough that I could probably still deflect them.

"Because I need you to listen to me," I said. "When you see the red bandanna hanging there, you stay away from the barn. Understand? You see red, you don't go near it."

"But why?"

Lilian put a hand on Justine's shoulder. She understood. I could see it in the tight set of her jaw, the way she wouldn't quite meet my eyes.

"Just trust Shane," Lilian said, her voice scratchy with unspoken pain. "If he says stay away, we stay away."

Hayley tugged on my shirt. At six, she was too young to understand the real danger, but old enough to follow instructions. "What about blue?"

"Blue means everything's fine. Normal. You can do your chores, go wherever you need to go."

"Like a game?" Her golden eyes lit up. "Red means stop, blue means go?"

"Exactly like that." I crouched down to her level. "But it's important, Hayley. Really important. If you see red and you need something from the barn, you come get me first. Understand?"

She nodded solemnly, blond hair bouncing. "I promise."

I looked at each of them in turn—Lilian, Justine, Hayley. Three girls who shouldn't have to understand warning systems and danger signals. Three girls I was responsible for keeping alive.

"Good," I said. "Now let's go over it again."

———

THE SYSTEM WORKED.

Two weeks later, I heard the whistle that meant the gang was coming in—one short blast, their all-clear signal. I was at the well, and by the time I got to the barn, four horses were already tied up outside. I didn't waste time checking who was inside. Just grabbed the red bandanna from my back pocket and hung it on the hook, then found work to do in the yard where I could keep an eye on both the barn and the house.

Twenty minutes later, Justine came out to hang laundry. She glanced at the barn, saw the red bandanna, and immediately changed direction. She dropped the basket and went back inside without ever getting close.

I felt something loosen in my chest. Relief, maybe. Or just the knowledge that one danger had been dealt with.

That night, I switched out the red for blue. By morning, the gang had ridden out again, and my sisters could move freely around the property.

It wasn't perfect. It didn't solve everything. But it was something.

After that, I built a clothesline on the other side of the house for our laundry so the girls wouldn't have to go near the barn.

———

SUMMER TURNED INTO fall, and the bandanna system became routine. Red meant danger; blue meant safe. My sisters learned to check the hook first thing every morning, learned to plan their days around that scrap of fabric hanging by the barn door.

I learned to read the signs of the gang's arrival with their dust on the horizon, the particular way the horses shifted in the corral when strangers were near, the change in the air that came before violence. I got faster at switching the bandannas, more strategic about positioning myself where I could watch without being obvious.

But the weight of it never got lighter.

Every time I hung that red bandanna, I thought about what I was protecting them from. Every time I saw Lilian glance at the barn with that haunted look in her eyes, I knew she understood more than I'd ever told her. Every time Caleb

Mason rode onto the property, I felt the helplessness of being fourteen and not strong enough to do anything but create warning systems and hope they were enough.

One night in late October, I was sitting on the porch steps, watching the sun set over the distant hills. The sky was painted in shades of orange and red, beautiful in a way that felt wrong given everything else about our lives.

Lilian came out and sat beside me. She said nothing for a long time, just sat there in the growing darkness, her hands folded in her lap.

"Thank you," she finally said. Her voice was quiet, almost lost in the evening breeze.

"For what?"

"For the bandannas. For..." She trailed off, swallowed hard. "For trying."

I didn't know what to say to that. Trying wasn't enough. It would never be enough. But it was all I had.

"I wish I could do more," I said.

She leaned her head against my shoulder, and I felt how small she was, how young we both were to be carrying this kind of weight.

"I know," she whispered. "I pray every day that God will protect us. That He'll keep you safe while you're keeping us safe."

I didn't tell her I'd stopped believing God was listening. Didn't tell her that every time I hung that red bandanna, I felt more alone than I'd ever felt in my life. She needed to believe someone bigger than a fourteen-year-old boy was watching over us.

Maybe she was right. Maybe someone was.

I just couldn't feel it.

——

WINTER CAME, AND with it, longer stretches when the gang was away. The blue bandanna hung on the hook for days at a time, and I almost let myself relax.

Almost.

But then I'd see the way Lilian flinched when a horse whinnied unexpectedly, or the way Justine's hands shook when she had to walk past the barn even when the blue bandanna was up. I'd see Hayley checking the hook three, four, five times before she'd venture near the barn, even on clear days.

The system protected their bodies. But it couldn't protect them from the fear, from the knowledge of what that red bandanna meant.

And it couldn't protect me from the crushing responsibility of being the one who decided when to raise the alarm, who had to be vigilant every moment of every day, who couldn't afford to make a single mistake.

I was fifteen years old by then. I'd been the man of the house for over two years. And some days, I wasn't sure how much longer I could hold it together.

But I would. Because they needed me to.

So I kept watch. Kept the bandannas ready. Kept my sisters as safe as a system of colored fabric and constant vigilance could keep them.

It wasn't enough.

But it was all I had.

Interlude - By The Fire

———————

THE FIRE HAS burned down to coals, and I realize I've been staring at them for a long time without speaking. My grandchildren are quiet, absorbing what I've told them.

"That was smart, Grandpa," Emma says finally. "The bandanna system."

"It was necessary," I correct gently. "There's a difference."

Tessa sets down her knitting. "You always had a choice, Shane. You could have left. Run away and saved yourself."

The grandchildren look shocked at the suggestion.

"No," I say firmly. "That was never a choice. Not for me. They were mine to protect. I'd made that decision the night I promised myself they'd all survive. Everything else followed from that."

"Even when it was hard?" Jake asks.

"Especially when it was hard." I lean back in my chair, feeling the ache in my bones that comes with age and old injuries. "And it got harder. Much harder. But I couldn't walk away. Wouldn't."

Emma is quiet for a moment, then asks the question that's probably been building in her mind since I started talking. "But Grandpa, who protected you?"

The question hits me like it always does, even after all these years. Who protected me? I was fourteen, fifteen, sixteen—just a kid myself, carrying the weight of keeping five other kids alive. Who was watching out for me?

I don't have an answer. Never have.

But Tessa does.

She leans over and puts her hand on my shoulder, warm and steady. I glance at her, and she gives me that look. The one that says she sees past all my walls, all my careful control, straight to the scared boy I used to be.

"God did," she whispers.

I nod slowly. Even now, it's hard for me to say it, hard to believe it some days. But looking back at those years, at the impossible situations we survived, at the narrow escapes and the times when everything should have fallen apart but somehow didn't...

Maybe she's right.

Maybe I was never as alone as I felt.

"God gave your grandfather wisdom beyond his years," Tessa continues, speaking to the children now. "A fourteen-year-old boy shouldn't have been able to think so strategically, to create systems that saved lives. But the Lord provides what we need when we need it, even when we don't recognize it as His provision."

"So God helped Grandpa think of the bandanna?" Emma asks.

"God gave your grandfather intelligence and creativity and the courage to use them," Tessa says. "Shane thought he was alone, but he never was. Not really."

I'm quiet, letting her words settle over the room. Even now, part of me resists the idea that I wasn't carrying everything by myself. That someone was holding me up when I felt like I was drowning.

But another part of me, the part that's learned to trust Tessa's faith even when my own is weak, knows she's speaking the truth.

"Your sister Lilian prayed for you," Tessa says, looking at me now. "Every single day, she prayed for all of you."

"She did," I admit. "She told me once that night on the

porch. I didn't believe it mattered then."

"But it did," Tessa says. "It does still."

I look at my grandchildren with their serious faces, their wide eyes taking in these stories of a childhood so different from their own secure, loving home. They need to understand both things: the darkness of what happened, and the light that somehow saw us through it.

"The bandanna system worked," I say finally. "It kept them safer than they would have been without it. But Tessa's right. I didn't come up with it on my own, even if I thought I did at the time. Something—Someone—was guiding me. Giving me what I needed to keep them alive."

"Even when you didn't believe?" Jake asks.

"Especially then," Tessa answers before I can. "God doesn't wait for us to believe before He acts. He just acts. And sometimes it takes us years to look back and see His hand in our story."

I nod, my throat tight. She's right. It took me decades to see it. Took meeting her, took learning to trust something bigger than myself, took finally letting go of the belief that I had to do everything alone.

But now I can see it. In the bandanna system that shouldn't have worked but did. In the narrow escapes and close calls where everything could have gone wrong but didn't. In the fact that all six of us survived when we had no right to.

God protected me.

Even when I didn't know it.

Even when I couldn't feel it.

He was there.

3 - Ike's Birthday

Summer 1885

THAT WAS THE year I stopped calling him Pa. He brought nightmares and destruction to our lives. Galen Harper. Outlaw. Nothing more.

I woke before dawn to Galen's gang stumbling into the barn. Six days now. Six days straight, and the world shrank smaller with every hour they stayed.

Flynn and Ike breathed steady beside me in the loft's darkness. Outside, five voices rose and fell. Galen's cut through the others—half-drunk, all mean. A successful run. Whiskey, poker, and a mood that sent my sisters vanishing into the house like rabbits into holes.

Ike shifted in his sleep. Seven years old in three days. Three days, and he'd never had a birthday that mattered. Never had a cake. Never had a gift wrapped in paper. Never had his family gather around him like he was someone worth celebrating instead of another mouth to feed.

I stared at the rough-hewn beams above my head and made a decision.

He was going to have one. Just one. Even if it killed me.

THE WOODEN HORSE already lay hidden in my bedroll, wrapped in an old shirt. Two months back, I'd found it half-buried in the barn dirt near the horse stalls. Some outlaw's idle carving, discarded and forgotten. The head was a little rough, one ear slightly crooked, but the legs stood sturdy and the mane had been carved with actual care.

I'd cleaned it with my knife, smoothed the splinters, rubbed it with saddle soap until it gleamed like polished walnut.

That was the easy part.

The hard part was everything else.

The gang cleared out that morning—off to scout another job, or nurse their hangovers in town, or whatever they did when they weren't making our lives miserable. Galen went with them. That gave me a window.

Lilian stood in the kitchen, trying to make something edible out of cornmeal and dried beans. Sixteen now, and this place showed in the tight line of her mouth, the way her hands never stopped moving.

"Ike's birthday is Thursday," I said.

Her hands stilled on the pot. She didn't look up. "I know."

"I want to do something for him."

"Shane—"

"Just listen." I kept my voice low. Flynn was outside with the younger ones, but sound carried in this house. "You remember Mrs. Penderson? The woman with the egg business?"

Lilian's eyes lifted to mine. "The one who bought Mama's sewing basket last year?"

I nodded. Before Ma died, she'd done beautiful needlework. Mrs. Penderson had admired it once, offered to buy a few pieces. After the funeral, when we were desperate, Lilian had sold the whole basket for three dollars. We'd eaten for two weeks on that money.

"I want you to go see her. Tomorrow." I pulled a small leather pouch from my pocket and set it on the table. The coins inside clinked soft. "Tell her we need sugar. Just enough for a small cake. Trade her whatever work you can—mending, washing, anything."

Lilian picked up the pouch. Her fingers trembled as she weighed it. "This is your hunting money."

"I know."

"Shane, if we need meat—"

"We'll manage." Hunt extra next week. Bring down two rabbits instead of one. Skip meals myself if necessary. "Ike needs this more than we need another rabbit stew."

Her teeth caught her lip. For a second her eyes shone wet, but Lilian didn't cry. Hadn't since Ma's funeral. She nodded once, sharp and determined.

"Flour too," she said. "I'll need flour. And maybe eggs if she can spare them."

"Whatever you can get."

"What about—" She glanced toward the barn, meaning Galen and his men. "They won't—"

"I'll handle it." The words came out harder than I meant them to. "Thursday morning, send Justine and Hayley to the creek for water. Tell them to take their time. Keep Flynn with you. I'll keep the gang away from the house."

"How?"

I met her eyes. "Don't ask me that."

Understanding flickered across her face, followed by something that looked like pain. She knew. Of course she knew. There was only one way to buy Galen's cooperation.

"Shane, you don't have to—"

"Yes, I do." I picked up the empty water bucket near the door. Needed something to do with my hands. "This is happening. Ike gets one birthday that matters. One day where he feels like he's worth something."

"He already—"

"He doesn't know that." My voice cracked. Just slightly. I cleared my throat, hardened it. "He's seven, Lil. He thinks this is normal. He thinks every kid grows up hungry and scared, watching his sisters hide in the root cellar every time strange men ride up. I can't fix all of it. But I can give him this one day."

Lilian stood, crossed to me, and gripped my arm. Her fingers dug in hard enough to hurt. "What's he going to ask you to do?"

"It doesn't matter."

"Shane—"

"It doesn't matter," I repeated. "Whatever it takes."

———

GALEN SAT IN the barn that afternoon, alone for once. He cleaned his rifle—a Winchester probably stolen from some unfortunate soul who'd crossed his path. He looked up when I walked in. His eyes narrowed.

"Something you need, boy?"

Boy. Like I was still thirteen and stupid enough to think he might actually be a father instead of a vulture picking at our family's corpse.

But I kept my face blank and my voice steady. "I need to make a deal."

He set down the rifle. Leaned back against the stall door. Galen liked deals. Liked the power of having something someone else wanted.

"What kind of deal?"

"Thursday morning, I need you and your men gone from the property. Whole day. Don't come back until after dark."

He laughed—short and mean. "You giving me orders now?"

"No sir." The words tasted like ash. "I'm asking for a favor."

"Favors cost, Shane. What're you willing to pay?"

Here it was. The moment I'd been dreading and planning for in equal measure.

"You've been talking about that ranch job over in Maricopa County. The one you need young blood for because it requires riding hard and fast."

His eyes sharpened. "I have."

"I'll do it. I'll ride with you."

The silence stretched between us, thick with implications. I'd never ridden on one of his jobs before. Never crossed that line from unwilling witness to active participant. Galen had pushed, occasionally, but I'd always found a way to refuse, to redirect, to make myself too valuable at the ranch to risk on his criminal schemes.

But he'd wanted this. Wanted to pull me into his world, make me complicit, turn me into what he was.

Now I handed it to him.

"Well." He set down his rifle, leaning back against the stall door. "Isn't that interesting. What's so important about Thursday that you're willing to sell your soul for it?"

"That's my business."

"It's my business if I'm granting favors." His smile was sharp as a knife blade. "What's Thursday?"

Lie. Should lie. But Galen would find out anyway, and then the deal would be off.

"My brother's birthday."

He stared at me. Then he threw back his head and laughed—loud and genuine, like I'd told him the funniest joke he'd ever heard.

"You're bargaining your conscience for a birthday party? For a seven-year-old kid?" He wiped his eyes. "Heck, Shane, you're softer than I thought."

Heat crawled up my neck. Soft. Like it was weakness. Like caring about a little boy's birthday made me less of what I needed to be. But any distinction between me and Galen's dark world was a good thing. Wasn't it? My fists stayed loose at my sides. My breathing stayed even.

"Do we have a deal or not?"

Galen studied me. His mind worked behind those calculating eyes, weighing options, figuring out how to extract maximum value from my desperation.

"Here's the deal," he said finally. "I'll clear out Thursday. Me and the boys will ride into town, won't come back until Friday morning. But when I say it's time for that Maricopa County job, you ride. No arguments. No excuses. No backing out. Understood?"

"Understood."

"And Shane?" His voice dropped lower. "Once you ride with us, you're one of us. There's no going back from that. You remember that while you're playing party games with your baby brother."

I met his eyes. "I'll remember."

"Good." He picked up his rifle again, dismissing me. "Thursday morning, we'll be gone by sunup. Better be worth it, boy."

I turned and walked out of the barn before he could see my hands shaking.

————

THURSDAY MORNING BROKE clear and hot. I was up before the sun, watching from the loft window as Galen and his men saddled their horses in the pre-dawn darkness. True to his word, they rode out just as the eastern sky started to lighten.

The dust from their horses settled. Then I climbed down the ladder.

The house transformed in their absence. Always did. Like a living thing that could finally breathe when the predators left. Lilian already stood in the kitchen, working on the cake with fierce concentration. The smell of sugar and flour—actual flour, not just cornmeal—filled the room like a promise.

"Justine and Hayley?" I asked.

"Sent them to the creek an hour ago. Told them to pick wildflowers on the way back." Lilian glanced up, a streak of flour on her cheek. "They'll be gone most of the morning."

"Where's Ike?"

"Out back with Flynn, feeding the chickens." Lilian's hands stilled on the mixing bowl. "Shane, I only had enough for a small cake. Just enough for Ike, Flynn, and Hayley."

"That's fine."

"You should have a piece. You're the one who—"

"No." I shook my head. "This is for them. The youngest ones. They need it more than we do."

She understood. The silent language of the two oldest, the two who carried everything so the others didn't have to.

"The wooden horse?" she asked softly.

I patted my pocket. "Got it."

———

THE PARTY WAS small. Simple. Nothing like what a real family would do, with neighbors and decorations and store-bought presents. But Ike's face when we called him inside and he saw the cake—tiny as it was, with one candle Lilian had saved from Christmas—made every compromise worth it.

"Is that for me?" His voice was small, awed.

"Happy birthday, Ike." I ruffled his hair, kept my voice light even though my chest squeezed tight. "Seven years old. That's a big deal."

Flynn bounced on his toes beside his brother, nine years old and still young enough to find joy in this. "Can we eat it now? Can we?"

"After he opens his present." Lilian appeared from the kitchen, wiping her hands on her apron. She caught my eye, nodded.

I pulled the wooden horse from my pocket and held it out to Ike.

He took it with both hands, reverent as a prayer. His fingers traced the carved mane, the sturdy legs, the slightly crooked ear that made it real instead of perfect.

"It's mine?" he whispered.

"It's yours."

"To keep?"

The innocent question gutted me. My throat worked. I choked out, "To keep forever."

Ike clutched the horse against him and threw his other arm around my waist. He shook—not crying, just overwhelmed by having something that belonged to him alone.

Over his head, I met Lilian's eyes. Tears streamed down her face, silent.

This was worth it. Whatever came next, whatever Galen made me do on that Maricopa County job—this moment was worth it.

———

THEY ATE THE cake slowly, savoring every crumb. I watched from the doorway, memorizing it. Ike held his wooden horse in one hand and ate with the other, never setting it down. Flynn made jokes, and the others rewarded him with giggles. Hayley, who'd returned from the creek with an armful of yellow flowers, wove them into a crown and placed it on Ike's head.

For two hours, we were almost normal.

Then the sun started sinking toward the horizon, and reality settled back over the house like a burial shroud.

"Bedtime," Lilian announced, though it was barely dusk. "Everyone upstairs."

The younger ones groaned but obeyed. They knew better than to argue when Lilian used that tone.

I followed them up to the loft and watched as Ike crawled into his bedroll, still clutching the wooden horse. His eyelids already drooped. Sugar and joy had worn him out.

"Shane?" he mumbled.

"Yeah, buddy?"

"This was the best day."

I smoothed the hair back from his forehead. "Good. You remember that."

"I'll remember forever." His eyes closed. "Forever and ever."

Within minutes, he was asleep, the wooden horse tucked under his chin.

I sat in the darkness, listening to my brothers breathe, and thought about Maricopa County.

Thought about the line I'd agreed to cross.

Thought about what it would cost—not the physical danger of the job, but the moral weight of it. The knowledge that I'd chosen to participate in evil so my baby brother could have one day of good.

Was it worth it?

Ike's sleeping face lay peaceful and safe in a way he so rarely was.

Yes. A thousand times, yes.

But that didn't mean it wouldn't leave scars.

Interlude - By The Fire

—————

THE FIRE CRACKLES in the hearth, filling the silence left by my story. Emma still holds her hand against her heart. Jake's eyes are wide, fixed on me like he's trying to understand something too big for his years.

"Did you have to do the bad job?" he asks finally. His voice wobbles. "The one you promised?"

"Yes." No point lying to him. "About a year and a half later, Galen called in the debt. I rode with them to Maricopa County. Helped them steal cattle from a ranch that couldn't afford to lose them."

"But you were helping Ike," Emma protests. "That makes it alright, doesn't it?"

Tessa sets down her knitting and leans forward. "No, sweetheart. It doesn't make it alright. It makes it understandable but not alright."

The children look confused. I don't blame them.

"Sometimes," Tessa continues, her voice gentle, "we face impossible choices. Your grandfather made one. He did something wrong for a right reason. The Bible talks about this. About how 'all have sinned and fall short of the glory of God.' Even when we're trying our best, even when we love people desperately, we're still broken people in a broken world."

"But God forgave Grandpa, right?" Jake asks.

"Eventually," I say. "Took me a long time to believe I deserved forgiveness. Longer still to accept it."

Tessa reaches over and squeezes my hand. "The beautiful part is this—that wooden horse your grandfather gave Uncle Ike? It still sits on his desk in his law office in Phoenix. He's forty-four years old now, a successful attorney, and he keeps that little carved horse right where he can see it every single day."

"Really?" Emma's face lights up.

"Really," I confirm. "I visited him last month. Asked him why he still had it after all these years. You know what he said?"

The children shake their heads.

"He said it reminds him that somebody thought he was worth sacrificing for. That even in the darkest time of our lives, when we had nothing and no one, his big brother gave up everything to make sure he knew he mattered."

Tessa nods. "That's the power of hope, children. Your grandfather planted hope in Uncle Ike's heart that day—hope that he was valuable, that he was loved, that someone would fight for him. And that hope grew into the man he is today."

"But it cost you," Jake says quietly, looking at me.

"It did," I admit. "Cost me pieces of my soul I didn't get back for years. That's the thing about impossible choices. They leave scars even when they're the right choice to make."

"Is that why you're telling us these stories?" Emma asks. "Because of the scars?"

Smart girl. Just like her mother, our Clara.

"I'm telling you because you need to understand what shaped your family. What made us who we are." I look between them. "And because the next story is harder than the birthday. Much harder. But it's part of the same thread. Doing whatever it takes to protect the people you love, even when it costs you everything."

Tessa stands and moves to stoke the fire. "Maybe that's enough for tonight—"

"No," Jake interrupts. "We want to hear it. Don't we,

Emma?"

She nods, still hugging her arms around her.

I take a breath and begin.

4 - The Impossible Choice

Winter 1887

A YEAR AND a half after Ike's seventh birthday, Galen called in the debt.

I'd known it was coming. Had felt it hanging over me like a storm cloud since the day I'd made that deal in the barn. But knowing didn't make it easier when he finally cornered me in the tack room on a February morning so cold my breath frosted in the air.

"Time to earn your keep, boy." He leaned against the doorframe, blocking my exit. "We ride out tonight."

My hands stilled on the bridle I'd been mending. "Where?"

"Maricopa County. Like I told you back in the summer." His smile was all teeth, no warmth. "You remember our deal?"

I remembered. Remembered every word, every implication, every compromise I'd made to buy Ike one day of happiness.

"I remember."

"Good. We leave at sundown. Dress warm. It's going to be a long night."

He walked away whistling, like he hadn't just pulled me deeper into his world of violence and theft. Like he hadn't just yanked the last shred of my integrity into the darkness with him.

I finished mending the bridle with hands that wanted to shake. Kept them steady through sheer will. Below in the house, I could hear Flynn's laughter. Ten years old and still capable of joy. Still innocent.

That's what I was protecting. That laughter. That innocence.

I had to keep telling myself that.

———

FIVE OF US rode out that evening—Galen, Bart, Caleb, Victor, and me. The brothers sat their horses with the easy confidence of men who'd done this a hundred times. Victor kept shooting me looks, amused and mean. He knew this was my first real job. Knew I was about to lose something I couldn't get back.

"Stick close, boy," Galen said as we headed west into the falling darkness. "Watch and learn. Tonight you become useful."

Useful. Like I was a tool. A weapon he'd been sharpening for years, finally ready to use.

The ride took three hours. Cold sank through my coat, and settled into my bones. Nobody talked much. Just the steady rhythm of hooves on frozen ground, the creak of leather, and the occasional snort from a horse.

We stopped at a ridge overlooking a small ranch. Lamplight glowed in the windows of a modest house. Smoke rose from the chimney. Peaceful. Normal.

"That's the Granger place," Galen said. "Frank Granger. Runs about three hundred head of cattle. Good stock. Easy pickings."

"Where's his hands?" I asked.

"In town for the weekend. Granger gave them time off." Galen's teeth flashed in the moonlight. "Generous man.

That generosity is going to cost him."

My stomach twisted. "We're taking his cattle?"

"That's the job."

"All of them?"

"As many as we can move fast." Galen looked at me. "You got a problem with that?"

Yes. I had a problem with destroying a man's livelihood. With stealing three hundred head of cattle from someone who'd probably worked his whole life to build that herd. But I also had Flynn back home, and Ike, and Hayley—still too young, still needing protection. Lilian and Justine too.

"No sir," I said. "No problem."

Galen's smile widened. "That's what I like to hear. Now, here's the thing, Shane. Granger's a problem. He's been talking in town. Asking questions. Mentioning how he's noticed cattle going missing in the area. Wondering if maybe someone ought to look into it."

A chill that had nothing to do with the February cold slid down my spine. "What are you saying?"

"I'm saying Granger needs to stop asking questions. Permanently."

The world spun. I gripped my saddle horn. "You want me to—"

"I want you to handle it." Galen's voice went flat, hard. "You're the one with steady hands and a good eye. You put a bullet in Frank Granger while we round up his cattle. Clean. Quick. Make it look like he surprised a rustler and got shot for his trouble."

"No." The word came out before I could stop it. "No, I won't—"

"You will." Galen leaned forward in his saddle. His eyes caught the moonlight, cold as a snake's. "Because if you don't, I'll send Flynn next time. Your brother's getting old enough for this kind of work. Might as well start him young."

The threat hit like a fist to the gut. Flynn. Ten years old. Still laughing, still playing, still thinking the world had good in it.

"You wouldn't."

"I would." Galen's voice was flat, certain. "And you know it. So you can either grow up tonight and do what needs doing, or you can watch me turn Flynn into what you're too soft to become."

I stared at him. At this man who'd sired me but never been a father. At the monster who'd destroy his own son's innocence just to prove a point.

"I'll do it," I heard myself say. My voice sounded distant, like it belonged to someone else. "I'll handle Granger."

"Good boy." Galen straightened. "Victor, you go with him. Make sure our young pup doesn't lose his nerve."

Victor's grin was sharp and eager. "Be my pleasure."

————

WE LEFT THE horses tied in a stand of cottonwoods and approached the house on foot. My rifle felt heavier than it ever had. Each step took effort, like walking through deep mud.

"Never killed a man before?" Victor whispered. He sounded excited.

"No."

"It's easier than you think. Just point and squeeze. Don't think about it too much."

But I was thinking. Couldn't stop thinking. Thinking about Frank Granger inside that warm house. Maybe reading. Maybe writing letters. Maybe just sitting by his fire after a long day of honest work. A man whose only crime was noticing cattle going missing and having the courage to mention it.

A good man.

And I was supposed to kill him.

We reached the side of the house. Through the window, I could see him—middle-aged, graying hair, wire-rimmed spectacles. He sat at a table writing something. His hand moved steadily across the page.

"There's your shot," Victor breathed. "Through the window. He'll never know what hit him."

I raised my rifle. Sighted down the barrel. Put Frank Granger's head in my sights.

My finger rested on the trigger.

One squeeze. That's all it would take. One squeeze and Flynn would be safe. One squeeze and Galen wouldn't have an excuse to pull my brother into this nightmare.

One squeeze.

I couldn't do it.

My hands shook. Sweat ran down my back despite the cold. The rifle sight wavered, blurred.

I couldn't do it.

"What's wrong?" Victor hissed. "Take the shot."

"I—" My voice cracked. "I can't—"

"Useless." Victor snatched the rifle from my hands. "Step aside, whelp. I'll show you how it's done."

He raised my rifle in one smooth motion. Sighted. Squeezed.

The shot cracked loud in the cold night air.

Through the window, Frank Granger jerked. His hand spasmed across the page. Then he slumped forward, head hitting the table with a sound I heard even through the glass.

Dead.

Just like that. One second alive and writing, the next second gone.

Victor lowered the rifle and handed it back to me. "See? Easy. Now let's move. The others will have heard that shot."

He jogged back toward the horses, unconcerned, like he'd just shot a coyote instead of a man.

I stood frozen, staring through the window at Frank Granger's body. Blood pooled on the table, soaking into whatever he'd been writing. His hand still held the pen.

What had he been writing? A letter to a friend? A journal entry? Plans for spring planting?

I'd never know. None of it mattered now.

"Shane!" Victor's hiss came from the darkness. "Move!"

I stumbled after him. My legs worked on their own, carrying me away from what I'd witnessed. What I'd been part of. What I'd enabled by being here, by making this deal, by thinking I could control Galen's evil by participating in it.

Behind us, cattle lowed in confusion as the others rounded them up. Frank Granger's herd. His life's work. Being stolen while his body cooled at his kitchen table.

————

THE RIDE BACK took forever and no time at all. We drove the cattle hard, pushing them through the night toward one of Galen's hidden holding areas. My hands did the work automatically cutting off strays, keeping the herd moving. But my mind stayed back at that ranch house.

Frank Granger's head hitting the table.

The sound of it. The finality.

Dawn was breaking when we finally stopped. The cattle milled in a box canyon, penned by natural rock walls. Galen was jubilant.

"Good night's work, boys. Real good." He clapped me on the shoulder. "You did fine, Shane. Real fine."

I'd done nothing. Hadn't pulled the trigger. Hadn't saved anyone. Hadn't even had the courage to refuse.

"Victor did the shooting," I said. My voice was hollow.

"Doesn't matter who pulled the trigger." Galen's grip on my shoulder tightened. "You were there. You're part of this now. Welcome to the family business."

Family business. Like murder was just another trade to pass down from father to son.

Bart Mason counted the cattle, tallying numbers in a small notebook. "Two hundred seventy-three head. Not bad."

"We'll rest them here a day, then move them south," Galen said. "Shane, you and Victor take first watch. The rest of us are heading back."

So I spent the morning watching stolen cattle with the man who'd murdered Frank Granger. Victor talked the whole time, bragging about other jobs, other men he'd killed, the best ways to make a shot count.

I stopped listening. Just watched the cattle and thought about my brothers and sisters back at the ranch.

Thought about how I'd bargained my soul to that devil Galen to protect them.

Thought about how it hadn't worked. Victor had pulled the trigger anyway. A man was dead anyway. And I was just as guilty as if I'd done it myself.

More guilty, maybe. Because I'd had a choice. Could have refused from the start. Could have taken whatever consequences came rather than making deals with a wicked outlaw.

But I'd been so sure I could manage it. Control it. Keep my family safe by being the one who dirtied his hands.

I'd been a fool.

———

WE GOT BACK to the ranch late that afternoon. Galen and the Mason brothers headed straight for the barn and the whiskey they kept hidden there. I went to the house.

Flynn met me at the door. His face lit up when he saw me. "Shane! Where've you been? I had to do all the morning chores myself."

"Sorry, buddy. Got pulled away for something."

"What something?"

"Nothing important." The lie tasted like ash. "You get the chickens fed?"

"Yeah, and I fixed that loose board in the corral like you showed me." Pride colored his voice. He wanted my approval. Wanted to show me he could handle responsibility.

I looked at my ten-year-old brother. Still small for his age. Still skinny from years of not quite enough food. Still innocent enough to be proud of fixing a fence board.

This was what I'd protected. This boy. This innocence. This trust in his big brother to keep him safe.

I couldn't keep him safe. Not from Galen. Not from the Mason brothers. Not from the pure evil that lived on our property and would eventually pull him in. Same way it had pulled me.

Because that's what I'd learned last night, watching Victor kill Frank Granger without hesitation or remorse. I'd learned that evil didn't negotiate. Didn't compromise. Didn't let you make deals that kept your family safe.

Evil just took. And took. And took.

And I couldn't fight it alone.

"Shane?" Flynn's voice pulled me back. "You alright? You look funny."

"I'm fine." I ruffled his hair, forcing a smile. "Just tired. Long night."

"You should rest."

"Maybe later." I looked past him into the house. Saw Hayley helping Lilian in the kitchen. Saw Ike playing with his wooden horse on the floor with Justine. My family. Not just my siblings anymore—my family. The people I was responsible for. The people I loved more than my own life. My own soul.

The people I couldn't protect by absorbing evil and hoping it would be enough.

A new thought crystallized, hard and clear as winter ice.

If I couldn't protect them from the darkness, I had to teach them to protect themselves.

Had to give them the tools, the skills, the ruthlessness to survive when I couldn't be there. When deals didn't work. When my best efforts failed.

I couldn't make Flynn into what I was becoming. That was what Galen wanted. But I could make Flynn dangerous enough that Galen wouldn't dare try.

Could teach Hayley to fight back against men like Victor.

Could train Ike to see threats coming.

Could turn them all into weapons that evil would think twice about touching.

The thought should have horrified me. Should have felt like failure. Like giving up on their innocence.

Instead, it felt like the first real strategy I'd had in years.

"Flynn," I said quietly. "You ever think about learning to fight? Real fighting, I mean. Not just wrestling."

His eyes widened. "Could you teach me?"

I taught him tracking, hunting, and survival. But Flynn needed to learn violence. Needed to learn it from someone who understood it but wasn't consumed by it. Yet.

"I'll think about it," I said. "Get back to your chores. We'll talk later."

He bounded off, energy restored by the prospect of something new to learn. I watched him go and made a mental plan.

Flynn would teach Hayley. I'd make him think it was his idea, make it a game between them. But I'd orchestrate it. Give them time. Make sure they had what they needed.

And I'd watch. Always watch. Always ready to step in if the real threats came.

But I'd stop trying to absorb all the evil myself. Stop making deals with the devil and thinking I could come out clean.

Last night had taught me the truth: I couldn't protect them from darkness by walking into it alone.

But I could teach them to be dangerous enough that darkness thought twice before coming for them.

————

THAT NIGHT, AFTER everyone was asleep, I sat in the loft watching Flynn and Ike sleep in the darkness. My rifle lay across my knees. I'd cleaned it three times already, trying to scrub away the memory of Victor using it to kill a good man.

The metal still felt tainted.

"They can hate me later," I whispered to the darkness. "As long as they're safe."

But safe didn't mean protected anymore. Safe meant armed. Trained. Dangerous.

Safe meant I'd failed to keep their innocence, but I'd succeed in keeping them alive.

It would have to be enough.

Interlude - By The Fire

_____

THE FIRE CRACKLES lower. No one speaks for a long moment. Emma's face is pale, her hands clenched in her lap. Jake stares at me like he's trying to reconcile the grandfather he knows with the young man who rode with killers.

"Grandpa?" Emma's voice is barely a whisper. "Were you... were you a bad man?"

Tessa starts to speak, but I raise my hand gently. It's a fair question. One I've asked myself a thousand times.

"I did bad things," I say carefully. "I rode with criminals. Helped them steal cattle. Stood by while an innocent man was murdered. Does that make me bad?" I pause, holding her gaze. "I've spent my whole life trying to answer that question."

"But you were trying to protect Uncle Flynn," Jake protests. "You didn't pull the trigger."

"I was there. That makes me guilty too." The words taste bitter, even after all these years. "Being there, doing nothing—that's a choice. A sin."

Tessa leans forward, her knitting set aside. "Your grandfather is right that what happened was sin. The Bible is clear—'all have sinned and fall short of the glory of God.' But Shane, you're also leaving something out."

I look at her, waiting.

"You couldn't pull the trigger," she says softly. "When

the moment came, when you had to choose between your brother's safety and an innocent man's life, you couldn't do it. Even knowing what it might cost Flynn, you couldn't murder that man."

"Victor did it anyway. Granger died anyway."

"Yes. But you didn't kill him. That matters." Her voice is gentle but firm. "You were trapped in an impossible situation by an evil man. You made the best choice you could see. And when it came down to it, you couldn't cross that final line."

Emma wipes her eyes. "It still hurt people though."

"Yes, sweetheart. That's the nature of sin. It spreads. It damages. Even when we're trying our best, even when we love people desperately, we're still broken people in a broken world. Romans 3:23 tells us that. But it doesn't stop there. Romans 6:23 says 'the wages of sin is death, but the gift of God is eternal life in Christ Jesus our Lord.'"

"God forgave you, right Grandpa?" Jake's voice is urgent, needing the reassurance.

"Eventually," I say. "Took me decades to believe I deserved forgiveness. Took meeting your grandmother"—I glance at Tessa—"to finally understand that God's grace is bigger than my failures."

"But that night changed everything," Tessa says, looking at the children. "Can you see it? Your grandfather realized he couldn't protect his family by absorbing all the evil himself. He had to give them tools. Teach them to defend themselves. That wisdom—that shift in thinking—probably saved all their lives."

"God used even that terrible night," I admit reluctantly. "Used it to show me I needed a different strategy. That's what the next stories are about. Teaching my family to be dangerous enough that evil thought twice."

Jake yawns suddenly, trying to hide it. Emma's eyes are drooping despite the intensity of the story.

"That's enough for tonight," Tessa says, standing. "You two need your beds. These are heavy stories for young hearts."

"But—" Emma starts to protest.

"Tomorrow," I promise. "There are more stories to tell. Harder ones, even. But they can wait until morning."

The children reluctantly stand. Jake gives me a fierce hug. "I'm glad you couldn't shoot him, Grandpa. I'm glad you couldn't."

Something tight loosens in my chest. "Me too, buddy."

Emma hugs me next, careful and gentle like she thinks I might break. "Thank you for telling us. Even though it's hard."

"Go on now. Off to bed."

They trudge upstairs, whispering to each other. Their footsteps fade. Doors close. Then it's just Tessa and me in the firelight.

She sits back down, picks up her knitting, but doesn't work on it. Just holds it. "That one cost you."

"They all do." I stare at the dying flames. "Not sure why I'm doing this. Dredging up things that should stay buried."

"Because they need to know." Her voice is firm. "Shane, you've always told them stories about being a Livestock Detective. About working as an Arizona Ranger. You made it sound like adventures—exciting, dangerous, but ultimately fun."

"It was, mostly."

"But that's not the whole story." She sets down her knitting and looks at me directly. "Those adventures were possible because of these years. Because of what God forged in you through darkness and impossible choices. The man who became an Arizona Ranger, who helped bring justice to the territory, who saved lives—he was shaped in a crucible of suffering."

I want to argue. Want to say it was just survival, just desperation. But I know she's right.

"Isaiah 48:10," she continues softly. "'Look, I have refined you, but not as silver; I have tested you in the furnace of affliction.' That's what those years were, Shane. God's

51

refining fire. It didn't feel like God at the time, did it?"

"No." The word comes out rough. "Felt like abandonment. Like being left to drown."

"But you weren't drowning. You were learning to swim in deep water. Learning strategy, patience, sacrifice. Learning to see what needed to be done and do it, even when it cost you everything." She reaches over and takes my hand. "Those lessons made you the man who could protect a widow and her children years later. Made you the Ranger who could see through lies when no one else could. Made you the husband and father you are today."

"Pretty painful way to learn."

"Most refinement is." She squeezes my hand. "But it's good for them to hear this. To understand that their grandfather—their strong, capable grandfather who always seems to know what to do—was once a terrified boy making impossible choices. To see that God uses our darkest moments to shape us into who we're meant to be."

I'm quiet for a moment, watching the embers glow. "There are harder stories coming. Much harder."

"I know." Her voice is steady. "Tell them anyway. They're old enough. And you need to tell them. You've carried these stories alone for too long."

She's right. Sharing them with Tessa over the years helped. Sharing them with Grady after the rescue helped. But telling my grandchildren—letting the next generation understand what shaped their family—this is different. Necessary, maybe.

"Tomorrow," I say finally. "I'll tell them about teaching them to fight. About what happened to Hayley when she had to use those skills."

"Good." Tessa stands, pulling me up with her. "But tonight, you rest. Come to bed. The stories will keep until morning."

I follow her upstairs, leaving the fire to burn itself out. Behind me, the shadows seem a little less heavy.

Tomorrow I'll tell them more. Tomorrow I'll show

them how God's refining fire burned away everything unnecessary, leaving only what was needed for survival and service.

Tonight, I'll sleep beside my wife in our warm, safe home, and thank God that those dark years led to this.

To my second family. To peace. To grace.

5 - Sparring Day

Summer 1888

I WATCHED FLYNN circle Hayley in the dust behind the barn, both of them slick with sweat in the brutal Arizona heat.

She was thirteen now. Old enough that men noticed her. Old enough that the Mason brothers had started watching her with the same calculating interest they'd shown Lilian and Justine years ago.

Old enough to learn how to fight back.

"Keep your weight centered," Flynn said, demonstrating the stance. He was eleven, nearly twelve, but already showing signs of the man he'd become. Lean muscle, quick reflexes, that edge of controlled aggression I'd been working to channel properly.

Hayley mimicked his posture, her face set with determination. She'd always been scrappy, willing to stand her ground, but that wasn't enough. Not against grown men who'd proven they had no conscience.

"Now come at me," Flynn instructed. "Remember what I showed you yesterday. Use my momentum against me."

She charged. Flynn sidestepped, caught her arm, and gently redirected her past him. She stumbled but caught herself.

"Again," he said.

I leaned against the barn wall, mending a bridle that didn't really need mending, my eyes tracking every movement. They'd been at this for three weeks now. Three weeks since I'd planted the seed with Flynn that Hayley needed to know how to protect herself.

He'd taken to the idea like he'd thought of it himself.

Smart kid. Dangerous, but smart.

———

IT STARTED A month before when Victor Mason cornered Hayley by the well.

I was in the barn, mucking stalls, when I heard her voice shift—not quite frightened, but wary. Careful. The tone that meant something was wrong.

I moved to the barn door.

Victor stood too close to her, one hand braced against the well's wooden frame, blocking her path. He wasn't touching her. Not yet. Just... looming. Testing. Seeing how she'd react.

Hayley stood her ground, chin up, but I saw the tension in her shoulders. She was trapped and she knew it.

I started across the yard, my hand instinctively moving toward the knife at my belt.

"Hayley!" Lilian's voice rang out from the house. "I need your help with this bread dough!"

Perfect timing. Lilian had seen it too.

Hayley ducked under Victor's arm and ran toward the house without looking back. Victor watched her go, then turned and saw me standing twenty feet away, knife loose in my hand.

He smiled. Tipped his hat. Walked back toward the barn where Bart waited.

But I'd seen it in his eyes. The decision forming. She was getting interesting to him. And Victor always took what he wanted, one way or another.

That night, after the younger kids were asleep, I found Flynn cleaning his rifle on the porch.

"Hayley's getting older," I said, settling onto the step beside him.

Flynn's hands stilled on the cleaning rod. "I know."

"You remember what happened with Lilian. With Justine."

His jaw tightened. "I remember."

Of course he did. Flynn forgot nothing, forgave less. Those memories had shaped him into something hard and unforgiving—something I was still trying to temper into a tool for justice instead of vengeance.

"Can't let that happen to Hayley," I said.

"No." His voice was flat. Final. "We can't."

I let the silence settle between us, let him think it through. Flynn was smart enough to see where this was going without me spelling it out.

"She needs to be able to fight," he said after a long moment.

"Yeah."

"Needs to know how to hurt someone. How to get away."

"Yeah."

He looked at me then, his young face aged beyond his years. "You want me to teach her."

"You're close enough in age. She'll listen to you. And..." I hesitated, choosing my words carefully. "She gets to keep thinking the world isn't as bad as it is. If I teach her, she'll know I'm desperate. If you do it, it's just... siblings looking out for each other."

Flynn nodded slowly, understanding the layers I wasn't saying. Keep her hopeful. Keep her from knowing just how much danger she was in. Let her think this was normal brother-sister stuff, not a last-ditch attempt to give her a chance against men twice her size.

"I'll do it," he said. "Starting tomorrow."

———

THAT FIRST SESSION was rough.

Flynn was too aggressive, pushing her too hard. Hayley fought back with pure stubbornness, but she didn't have the training yet, didn't know where to strike or how to twist away from a hold.

I watched her hit the ground for the fifth time and saw the frustration building in her face.

"Enough," I called out, crossing the yard toward them.

Both of them looked up, startled. I'd been careful to keep my distance, to let Flynn think this was his project, but I couldn't watch her get discouraged and quit before she learned what she needed.

"Flynn, show her slow," I said. "Break it down. She's got to learn the movements before she can use them."

Flynn wiped sweat from his face. "I am showing her."

"You're showing her how *you* fight. She's not built like you. She's got to use different tactics." I turned to Hayley. "You're faster than him. Lighter. Use that. Don't try to over-power. Outsmart."

Hayley's eyes lit up with understanding. "Like when I beat Ike at checkers."

"Exactly like that." I demonstrated a hold, moving slowly so she could see the mechanics. "When someone grabs you here, you don't pull straight back. They're expecting that. You twist this way, toward their thumb. Weakest point in the grip."

She tried it on Flynn's arm. He held firm, and she twisted, and suddenly she was free.

"Oh," she breathed. Then a grin split her face. "Oh!"

"Do it again," Flynn said, catching the teaching method now. "Ten times, until your body knows it without thinking."

I stepped back and let them work.

Over the following weeks, I watched Hayley transform. She learned to fight dirty—eyes, throat, groin. The vulnerable places that could drop a man regardless of size difference. She learned to use her elbows, her knees, her forehead. Learned how to fall without getting hurt, how to roll and come up ready.

Flynn taught her knife work too. Basic stuff at first— how to hold it, how to open a folding blade fast, where to cut to make someone let go without killing them.

"Only if you have to," Flynn told her seriously. "But if you have to, don't hesitate."

She nodded, her face solemn, and I saw the last traces of childhood innocence fade from her eyes.

The cost of survival. Always the cost.

———

AUGUST BROUGHT THE test I'd been dreading.

Lilian and Justine had gone to town for supplies. I was working in the north pasture, far enough from the house that I couldn't see the yard. Flynn had taken Ike fishing at the creek.

Hayley was alone.

I realized it halfway through checking fence posts, and fire burned my gut. Wrong. This was wrong. I'd gotten complacent, letting my guard down because the sparring sessions had been going well.

I abandoned the fence and ran for the house.

Got there in time to see Victor backing Hayley toward the barn, his bulk blocking her retreat. She'd been drawing water from the well. The bucket lay on its side, water darkening the dust.

"Just want to talk," Victor was saying, his voice thick with false friendliness. "Get to know you better."

I was fifty yards out, too far to reach her before he did.

But Hayley didn't wait for rescue.

When Victor reached for her arm, she moved. Twisted toward his thumb like Flynn'd taught her, broke his grip, and drove her knee into his gut. Not hard enough to drop him—she wasn't strong enough for that—but enough to make him stagger back a step.

Enough to create distance.

She ran.

Not toward the house. Toward the barn, where I knew she'd stashed one of Flynn's old knives in a feed sack. Smart girl. Going for a weapon instead of trying to outrun him.

Victor cursed and went after her.

I was thirty yards out, my boots pounding hard-packed earth, hand already on my knife.

Then Flynn appeared from around the barn corner.

He must have seen it from the creek path. Must have run flat-out to get here. He stepped between Victor and the barn door, and despite being eleven years old and half Victor's size, there was nothing childish in his stance.

"Back off," Flynn said, his voice deadly calm.

Victor stopped. Laughed. "Or what, boy?"

"Or Shane puts a bullet in you." Flynn jerked his chin toward me.

Victor turned and saw me bearing down on him, saw the knife in my hand and whatever expression was on my face that made grown men reconsider their choices.

He raised his hands, stepping back. "Just fooling around. No harm meant."

"Fooling's done," I said, my voice colder than I'd meant it. "You touch her again, I don't care what Galen says. You're done."

Victor's eyes went flat and dangerous. We stared at each other across ten feet of dust and heat and unspoken threats.

Then Bart called from the barn. "Victor! Let's go!"

Victor backed toward his horse, keeping his eyes on me the whole time. "This ain't over, Shane."

"Yeah," I said. "It is."

He rode out with Bart, dust rising behind them.

I turned to my siblings. Flynn stood rigid, fists clenched, rage barely contained. Hayley leaned against the barn door, breathing hard, her face pale but determined.

"You did good," I told her. "Both of you."

Hayley nodded, still catching her breath. Then, whispered, "I was going for the knife."

"I know."

"Would I have used it?"

The question hung in the summer air. I looked at my thirteen-year-old sister, saw the fear and determination warring in her eyes, and knew she deserved the truth.

"I hope you never have to find out," I said. "But yeah. If you had to, you would've."

She absorbed that, then straightened her shoulders. "Flynn. Tomorrow we train harder."

Flynn's fierce grin matched her expression. "Tomorrow we train harder."

———

September came, and with it cooler temperatures and news that Victor Mason had left Arizona Territory. Warrant trouble in New Mexico, someone said. Gone for months, maybe longer.

I watched Flynn and Hayley spar in the late afternoon sun, their movements more fluid now, more confident. She'd gotten faster, more aggressive. Knew where to hit to make it count.

She also laughed when Flynn let her win a round. Still braided Justine's hair. Still played with Ike and made up stories about the stars.

She got to keep some of herself. Not all of it—never all of it in this place—but enough.

Flynn called a break, and they both collapsed in the shade, passing a canteen between them. Partners now. Equals in a way they hadn't been before.

"They're good together," Lilian said from behind me.

I turned. My sister stood in the doorway, watching the

same scene I was.

"Yeah," I said.

"You orchestrated this. The training."

It wasn't a question. Lilian had always seen through me.

"They needed it," I said simply.

"I know." She was quiet for a moment. "I wish... I wish I'd known how to fight back. When Caleb..."

"I know." My throat tightened. "I'm sorry."

"Don't be." She looked at me, and I saw forgiveness in her eyes for failures I'd never stop punishing myself for. "You did what you could. You're still doing it. And Hayley..." She watched our sister laugh at something Flynn said. "Hayley has a chance we didn't."

I nodded, unable to speak past the weight in my chest.

Lilian squeezed my shoulder, then went back inside.

I stood there as the sun sank lower, watching my siblings spar and laugh and prepare for violence they shouldn't need to face but would anyway.

Tomorrow I'd teach Flynn more advanced techniques. Show him how to teach Hayley knife fighting properly, not just the basics. Make sure she knew how to be lethal if she had to be.

Tonight, I'd count it as a victory that she could still laugh.

One day at a time. One small protection at a time.

Keep them alive, whatever it took.

That was the job. That was everything.

Interlude - In The Kitchen

———————

THE AFTERNOON SUN slants through the kitchen windows. Tessa moves around the room, preparing lunch. The familiar rhythm of chopping vegetables, the sizzle of meat in the pan. The grandchildren sit at the table with me, still thinking about the morning's stories.

"Grandpa," Jake says slowly, "you made Uncle Flynn think teaching Aunt Hayley was his idea. But it was really yours."

"It was."

"That's kind of sneaky."

I chuckle. "Strategic. There's a difference."

Emma traces patterns on the worn wood of the table. "But why didn't you just tell him to do it? You were in charge."

"Because Flynn needed to own it. Needed to feel like he was protecting his sister, not just following orders. That made him a better teacher. Made him invested."

Tessa glances over from the stove. "Your grandfather understood something important. People fight harder for what they choose rather than what they're told to do."

"Is that why you and Grandma taught Mama and Uncle Jude to fight?" Emma asks. "So they could choose?"

The question catches me off guard. I exchange a look with Tessa.

"You know about that?" I ask carefully.

"Mama showed me once," Emma says. "How to get away if someone grabs my wrist. She said you taught her when she was little."

Jake nods. "Uncle Jude showed me how to punch properly. Said Grandpa made him practice on a flour sack until his knuckles were tough."

Tessa sets down her knife and comes to sit with us. "Your grandfather and I made a choice when Clara and Jude were young. We decided they needed to know how to defend themselves. But they also needed to understand why."

"What do you mean?" Jake asks.

I lean forward, choosing my words carefully. "When I was young, I learned to fight because I had to. Learned to be dangerous because dangerous men surrounded us. But I never learned the reason behind it. Was never taught that violence should be the last resort, not the first response."

"You just knew you had to survive," Emma says.

"Exactly. But when your mama and uncle were growing up, we had the chance to teach them differently. We taught them how to throw a punch, how to break a hold, how to use a knife if necessary. But we also taught them that every life has value. Even the life of someone trying to hurt you."

Tessa picks up the thread. "We taught them that defending yourself doesn't mean you stop seeing your attacker as a human being. It means you recognize that your life is valuable too. That God gave you the right to protect the life He created in you."

"The sanctity of life," I say. "That's what we called it. Every person is made in God's image. Including you. So you fight to preserve that image, not to destroy it."

Jake frowns, thinking. "But what if you have to kill someone? To stay alive?"

"Then you carry that weight. You don't celebrate it. You don't make it easy in your mind. You recognize the gravity of taking a life, even in defense of your own."

"Is that in the Bible?" Emma asks.

"Not exactly those words," Tessa says. "But the principle is there. 'Thou shalt not murder.' Not 'thou shalt not kill.' There's a difference. Murder is taking life without just cause. But defending the innocent, protecting your family... that's different."

I watch my grandchildren absorb this. "That's why we didn't just teach your parents to fight. We taught them wisdom. Discernment. When to act and when to walk away. When to show mercy and when to stand firm."

"The book of James says, 'Now if any of you lacks wisdom, he should ask God—who gives to all generously and ungrudgingly—and it will be given to him,'" Tessa quotes softly. "That's what your grandfather taught his family. Not just self-defense, but wisdom. How to think, how to choose, how to live."

"And Lilian made sure they knew where true wisdom came from." My voice roughens slightly. "She never stopped praying. Never stopped reading Scripture to us, even when I wanted nothing to do with it. She made sure my siblings understood that God was the source of wisdom, of strength, of everything good we had."

"But you didn't believe that then," Jake says. It's not a question.

"No. I thought I was the source of everything. Thought survival depended on my strategies, my plans, my ability to think three steps ahead." I shake my head. "Took me a long time to see that God had been giving me that wisdom all along. Every strategy that worked, every plan that saved them, every moment of insight that kept us alive... that was God answering Lilian's prayers, even when I didn't know enough to pray myself."

Tessa reaches over and squeezes my hand. "But you learned. And when you had children of your own, you made sure they understood from the beginning what took you decades to see."

"That's right. I taught Clara and Jude to defend themselves, but I also taught them to pray. Taught them that wisdom comes from God, and if they needed it, they should ask for it. James says God gives generously without finding fault. He doesn't hold it against us that we need His help."

"Did it work?" Emma asks. "Did God give them wisdom when they asked?"

I smile. "Your mama's still alive, isn't she? Still raising you well? That's not luck or coincidence. That's answered prayer. Wisdom applied. God's provision."

"So all those stories you're telling us," Jake says slowly, "they're not just about fighting and surviving. They're about learning to trust God for wisdom."

"Took me years to get there. But yes, that's the deeper story. How God took a terrified boy who thought he was alone, gave him the wisdom to keep his family alive, and then slowly, patiently, showed him that he'd never been alone at all."

Tessa stands and returns to the stove. "That's why these stories matter, children. Not just because they're your family history, but because they show how God works. How He shapes us, provides for us, teaches us. Even when we don't recognize His hand."

"Are there more stories?" Emma asks. "About Aunt Hayley and Uncle Flynn?"

"Several more. Harder ones. But also ones that show how God's wisdom kept working through impossible situations. How He prepared my family not just to survive, but to become who He created them to be."

"After lunch?" Jake asks hopefully.

I glance at Tessa. She nods, smiling.

"We'll continue after lunch. I'll tell you about the night Hayley had to use everything Flynn taught her. About what it cost her and what it proved."

The children seem satisfied with that. They drift away to help set the table, to do their evening chores. Tessa and I remain in the kitchen's warmth.

"You're doing well with this," she says. "Sharing the hard parts. The faith parts."

"Feels important. Want them to understand that strength without wisdom is just violence. And wisdom without God is just human cleverness, which fails eventually."

"It does." She returns to her cooking. "But wisdom from God? That endures. That's what kept your first family alive. And it's what built your second family too."

I sit in the afternoon light, watching my wife work, listening to my grandchildren's voices in the next room.

She's right.

Everything good I have came from wisdom I didn't know I was receiving. From a God I didn't know was listening. From prayers I was too stubborn to pray but Lilian prayed for me.

After lunch, I'll tell them more. I'll show them how that wisdom played out in darker moments, harder choices.

But for now, I sit in the warmth of my kitchen and thank God for the patience to wait for a stubborn man to finally see the truth.

6 - Hayley's Point

———————

Early 1890

I SPOTTED VICTOR Mason the moment he rode into the yard with Galen's crew. Recognized the way he sat his horse, the tilt of his hat. My gut clenched.

He'd been gone nine months. Long enough I'd hoped he wouldn't come back.

Should've known better.

Victor swung down from his saddle, moving like a man who'd healed from something painful. Word was he'd spent weeks recovering in Tucson. Broken ribs. Punctured lung from where he'd landed on something sharp at the bottom of the well.

Hayley had put him there. Fifteen years old and already dangerous when cornered.

But Victor wouldn't see it that way. He'd think she'd got lucky.

I watched him scan the yard, gaze settling on the house. Looking for her.

My hand drifted to my knife. Then stopped.

This was the moment Flynn's training would prove it-self. Either Hayley could handle Victor, or everything I'd built would collapse.

I had to let her try.

But I'd be close. Just in case.

———

I SHADOWED HER all morning. Stayed within thirty yards, kept obstacles between us so she wouldn't notice. She went about her chores—feeding chickens, hauling water, mending fence wire—while I tracked her like prey.

Hated doing it. Hated that it was necessary.

But Victor was watching her too. I saw him leaning against the barn, pretending to clean his rifle while his eyes followed every move she made.

Waiting.

Around noon, Hayley headed for the barn. Needed to fork hay down from the loft for the horses.

Victor straightened. Glanced around the yard. Then followed her inside.

My heart kicked against my ribs.

I crossed the distance in seconds, pressed myself against the barn wall near a gap in the boards. Close enough to hear. Close enough to act.

"Well, well." Victor's voice carried through the wood. "Little Hayley Harper. All grown up."

"Get away from me." Her voice was steady. Controlled. Like Flynn had taught her.

"Don't be like that. We're just talking."

"We're not talking. You're leaving."

"Not yet." Movement. Footsteps. "See, I've been thinking about you while I was laid up. Thinking about how you got lucky that day at the well. How next time, things might go different."

Through the gap, I saw him move closer. Saw Hayley back toward the ladder, hand sliding to her belt.

Where she kept her knife.

My muscles coiled. Ready to burst through that door.

But I held.

Waited.

Trusted.

"I said get away from me." Hayley's hand closed around the knife handle.

Victor lunged.

She moved like water. Sidestepped his grab, pivoted, drove the blade up under his ribs exactly where Flynn had shown her. Not deep enough to kill. Deep enough to make a point.

Victor's howl tore through the barn, laced with curses.

He staggered back, hand clutching his gut. Blood welled between his fingers. His face went white.

I shoved through the door.

Victor's eyes found me, wide with shock and pain. "You—you were—"

"Right here." I kept my voice flat. Walked past him to Hayley. "You alright?"

She nodded. The knife hung loose in her hand, blood dripping from the tip. Her face had gone pale but her jaw was set.

"Good." I turned to Victor. "Sit down before you fall down."

He sank against a hay bale, breathing hard. The wound wasn't fatal. Hayley had known exactly where to strike. Painful but survivable.

I crouched in front of him, met his eyes. "You're going to live. But you're going to remember this day. Remember that the younger Harpers aren't easy targets anymore. Touch any of them again, and next time the knife goes deeper. Understand?"

He nodded, teeth gritted against the pain.

"Shane?" Hayley's voice was small. "Is he—"

"He'll live." I stood, put myself between her and Victor. "Go to the house. Send Lilian out with bandages and whiskey. Then stay inside."

She didn't argue. Just turned and walked out, still holding that bloody knife.

I watched her go, my chest tight with pride and guilt in equal measure.

———

BY THE TIME I'd bandaged Victor enough that he wouldn't bleed out, Galen had appeared. He took one look at his man and shook his head.

"Told you to leave her alone."

Victor said nothing. Just pressed a hand to his side and glared.

"Get him out of here," I said. "And don't bring him back."

Galen studied me for a long moment. Then nodded. "Fair enough."

They loaded Victor onto his horse and rode out. I stood in the yard and watched them disappear into the heat shimmer on the horizon.

Inside, I found Hayley at the kitchen table. She'd washed the knife and her hands, but I could still see the tremor in her fingers.

Lilian had made tea. Justine sat beside Hayley, holding her hand.

I pulled up a chair across from her. "You did good."

"I stabbed him." Her voice shook. "I could've killed him."

"But you didn't. You controlled it. Used exactly the force you needed and no more." I leaned forward. "That's what Flynn taught you. How to be dangerous without being a killer."

"It felt—" She swallowed hard. "I wanted to go deeper. Wanted to make sure he couldn't—"

"I know." And I did. Knew that rage, that need for certainty. "But you didn't. That's what matters."

She looked at me then, really looked. "You were there the whole time. Weren't you?"

"I was."

"Why didn't you stop him before—"

"Because you needed to know you could handle it yourself." The words came out harder than I meant them. "If I'd stepped in, you'd always wonder. Always doubt. This way, you know. You're capable. You're strong. You're safe."

Tears spilled down her cheeks. "I don't feel safe. I feel—"

"Different," I finished. "I know. That's the cost."

She nodded, wiping at her face.

I wanted to tell her it would get easier. That the weight of what she'd done would fade.

But I'd never lied to my siblings, and I wasn't starting now.

"You'll carry this," I said instead. "But you're alive to carry it. Victor won't touch you again. That's worth something."

"Is it?" Her voice was barely a whisper.

I thought about all the things I carried. All the choices I'd made, and the lines I'd crossed.

"Yes," I said. "It is."

Later that night, after everyone had gone to bed, I sat outside and stared at the stars.

My strategy had worked. Hayley was safe. Victor had learned his lesson.

But the look in her eyes—that knowledge of what she was capable of—would never leave her.

I'd given her the tools to protect herself.

And in the process, I'd taken something she could never get back.

Interlude - On The Porch

———————

THE AFTERNOON'S SUN slants across the porch. Emma's fallen asleep against my shoulder, worn out from the weight of these stories. Jake sits quietly, chewing on that.

Tessa sets down her knitting. "You did the right thing, Shane."

I shake my head. "Did I? I let Victor corner her. Let her have to use violence. She was fifteen."

"She was fifteen and alive," Tessa says firmly. "Because you prepared her. Because you trusted her training when the moment came."

"She was just a girl."

"A girl who'd grown up in a house with dangerous men," Tessa counters. "You didn't put that evil there, Shane. You just gave her a way to survive it."

Jake leans forward. "Aunt Hayley's okay now, right? I mean, she's strong. A Pinkerton detective."

"She is," I confirm. "Married to a good man. Has beautiful children. Built a good life."

"Because of what you taught her," Tessa adds. "You've carried guilt over this for decades. But have you ever asked Hayley if she regrets learning to fight?"

I haven't. Been too afraid of the answer.

"She doesn't," Tessa continues. "I've talked to her about it. She told me that day in the barn was terrifying, but it was also the day she realized she wasn't helpless. That she could protect herself. That she didn't have to be a victim."

The words hit harder than I expect.

"You gave her agency," Tessa says. "Choice. Power over her own body and her own safety. Yes, it cost her innocence. But it saved her life. Would you rather she'd stayed innocent and died?"

"No." The word comes out rough.

"Then stop punishing yourself for protecting her the only way you could." She reaches over, takes my hand. "You weren't God. You were a twenty-three-year-old trying to keep his family alive with limited options and no help. You did the best you could."

"The best I could still left scars."

"All protection leaves scars. Even God's protection often comes with cost. But that doesn't make it less valuable." She squeezes my hand. "It was one of the ways God protected her. Because, Shane, she was never yours to protect fully. Only God's."

The truth of it settles into my chest. I'd tried to be everything—father, protector, provider, shield. Tried to keep them all safe through my own strength and planning.

But I couldn't be God. Could only do what I could do.

And sometimes, that meant teaching them to protect themselves.

"Hayley's alive," Tessa says again. "Thriving. Whole. Because you gave her what she needed when she needed it. That's not something to regret."

Jake speaks up then. "Grandpa, did Victor ever come back?"

"No. He learned his lesson. Stayed away from all of us after that." I look at my grandson. "Sometimes the only language dangerous men understand is danger. Hayley spoke it that day, and he heard her loud and clear."

"Good," Jake says fiercely.

Tessa smiles. "Your grandfather taught all his siblings to be dangerous to evil people. That's the Harper legacy. Not victims, but protectors. Not helpless, but capable."

I think about Hayley now. How she tracks down criminals. How she fights for justice. How she's teaching her own daughter to be strong.

Maybe Tessa's right. Maybe the cost was worth it.

"The next story gets darker still," I warn them. "It's about the breaking point. About the day I almost became the thing I was fighting against."

Emma stirs against my shoulder. "We're ready, Grandpa."

"Tomorrow," Tessa decides, standing. "These stories are heavy enough without rushing through them. Let's have dinner, and tomorrow we'll continue."

As they head inside, I sit in the fading light and think about Hayley's knife. About the blood on the blade. About the look in her eyes afterward.

And for the first time in thirty years, I let myself believe that maybe—just maybe—I made the right choice that day.

Even if it cost us both something we couldn't get back.

7 - Don't Become Him

Spring 1892

THE RICH AROMA pulled me from sleep. I donned my clothes and crept down the stairs, careful not to wake the others.

There Lilian sat at the table. Coffee already brewed hours before the house normally stirred. Two mugs. She nudged one closer to the empty chair at the head of the table. Her eyes looked anywhere but at me.

The soft glow of the lamplight cast strange shadows across her face. She folded her arms over her middle like she was holding something precious.

Something was wrong.

I settled into the chair. Sipped the bitter coffee. Nasty taste after the grounds being brewed so many times.

When she finally spoke, her voice was quiet, but steady.

"I'm pregnant."

The words sliced through me. I'd known I'd failed to protect her. More than once. Guilt gnawed at my conscience like a coyote hunting its prey.

I didn't speak right away. Just looked at her. She didn't flinch. Didn't look away. I saw the truth in her eyes before she said the rest.

"It's Caleb's."

I nodded once. Felt the weight crush my soul like a boulder.

A baby.

It changed things. Not just for her. For all of us. This place was no place for another innocent child to be born. Not with Galen Harper still breathing. Not with Caleb Mason still walking free. But we'd figure it out. We always did. I'd protect her. I'd protect the baby. No matter what it cost.

Find a way to feed another mouth. Preserve another child's innocence.

"About three months along." Her hand rested over her abdomen.

"God will provide," she added. "He always does."

Even if I didn't see it—didn't agree with it—I never squelched her hope in Him. It kept her sane. Gave her the strength to mother our younger siblings.

I ran a hand through my hair, drained my coffee, and stood.

"Best get started on the chores."

Then I left the house as if it were any day and not the day that'd change things again.

———

THEN CAME THE day I nearly lost my soul.

About a month later. Galen and his gang were in residence again. Lilian had started showing. Hard not to with her frame boney from years of neglect. The times she sacrificed a meal for the others. I'd done myself more times than I could count. I'd have to see she stopped doing that. For the baby's sake.

I was out in the field, checking the fence line where the cattle kept testing the wire. Sun beating down on my back for the better part of the day. When I finished, I headed back to the main house. Proud to see Flynn had put up the red bandanna. And relieved to see my family had stayed indoors.

I opened the door, and the house immediately felt wrong. Quiet, but not peaceful. Like death and darkness had paid a visit.

Justine was cooking, but her hands shook. Hayley sat with Ike, teaching him to sound out words from the Bible. Flynn was at the table, jaw clenched, eyes burning. He stood, brushing past me.

"Doing chores," he muttered, and slammed the door behind him.

I looked around again.

"Where's Lilian?" I asked.

Justine turned, tears already falling. Her voice broke. "In bed."

My heart rammed against my rib cage as I took the stairs two at a time. The door slammed against the wall. She sucked in a sharp breath at the loud noise. So did I, at the sight of her.

Her face was a mess. Bruises like ink stains. Her arms trembled.

My jaw tightened. I wanted to look away. Couldn't.

"He do this?" I asked.

"Shane." Her voice was thin, but steel ran under it. "Come here."

I stepped closer. Tear tracks cut through the bruises like rivers through scorched earth. Her eyes held wreckage. And something else.

"Baby is gone."

The words gutted me. I couldn't breathe. My chest burned. Rage surged—hot, vile, righteous. I was going to kill him. Caleb Mason had taken an unborn life. He'd shattered Lilian. Again. Again. Again.

I turned, ready to storm out, but her hand shot out—clamped around my wrist with a strength that didn't belong to someone so broken.

"Don't do it."

I tried to rip free. She held on like her soul depended on it.

"Don't become him."

Her voice was low, but it cut deep. Galen. That's who she meant. The man who taught Caleb how to break things that didn't fight back. The man who carved monsters from boys and found sick pleasure in it.

I didn't speak. Didn't nod. Just turned. The growl came from somewhere deep—animal, not human. I stormed out, boots pounding the floorboards like war drums. Winchester heavy in my hand. Toward the barn.

The backroom door slammed open. Caleb sat there, sharpening a blade like it was any other day. Like he hadn't just murdered something sacred.

I leveled the rifle. Sighted his chest. My finger curled around the trigger.

"You got one chance," I said. "Speak your sins."

He looked up. Smirked. "Ain't got none."

That was it. The last straw. The last breath of mercy I had left.

Don't become him.

The words clawed at my conscience, but I didn't care. Not then.

I wanted to squeeze the trigger. Wanted it more than I'd ever wanted anything. Let my soul rot. Let God turn His face. Let the gates of hell swing wide and welcome me home.

Because Caleb Mason didn't deserve another breath.

Then, arms of iron from behind. The rifle slipped, lowering out of sight but still pointed at Caleb enough to do some damage. Steel kissed the side of my neck, cold and sharp.

Victor.

"Drop it," he growled in my ear.

I tried to wrench free. The blade bit deeper. Warm blood trickled down my neck.

"I said, drop it."

Caleb stood slowly, blade still in hand, watching with the same sick smirk.

"Let him go." Galen's voice cut through the barn like a

whip crack.

I froze. Victor's grip didn't loosen.

Galen stepped into the doorway, hand hovering near his holster. His eyes locked on Victor. "You ain't spilling Harper blood on my land."

Confusion hit me like cold water. My blood? Caleb wasn't his blood. I was.

Victor shifted his stance, blade still pressed to my throat. "He ain't spilling *my* brother's blood either."

The air snapped tight. I could feel the heat off Victor's breath. The cold calculation in Galen's eyes. Two predators. One line.

Galen's hand twitched toward his ivory-handled six-shooter. "You want to challenge me, boy? You think I won't cut you down for crossing me?"

Victor didn't blink. Didn't lower the knife. "You think I won't do the same?"

The barn fell silent except for my pulse hammering against Victor's blade. Caleb stood frozen, watching the men who owned his fate.

Galen's jaw worked. Then something shifted in his eyes—not mercy, but calculation. He exhaled slowly, like letting go of something sharp.

"Stand down," he said. "Both of you."

Victor hesitated. The blade pressure eased slightly but didn't leave my throat.

Galen's voice dropped low. Menacing. Deadly. "I said stand down."

Victor stepped back. The knife disappeared. I sucked in air, hand flying to my neck where blood still trickled.

Galen turned to me. His eyes held something I'd never seen before. Not love. Not regret. Something harder to name.

"Get out!"

I didn't argue. Didn't speak. Just grabbed my rifle and walked out.

My neck burned where the blade had kissed it. My

hands shook with rage I couldn't spend. Even Galen—Galen—had stopped me from taking what was mine to take.

I didn't understand it then. Wouldn't understand it for years.

But Lilian did.

As I walked back toward the house, I rubbed the spot on my neck where Victor's knife had nicked me. Still confused. Still burning. Even Galen wouldn't let me be murdered. Made no sense.

Back at the house, the air was thick. My family sat around the table. Heads bowed. Hands clutched. Whispers meant for God alone.

At the center sat Lilian. Her face still bruised. Her body still broken. But her voice—steady. Leading them in prayer.

She didn't look up when I entered. Didn't flinch. Just kept praying.

I stood there watching her. The woman who had every reason to hate the world. Every reason to give up. And still—she prayed. For me.

It was Ike who saw me first.

"Shane! I prayed they wouldn't kill you."

The words hit like a hammer to the chest. I'd been the one ready to kill. Ready to die for it.

I stepped closer. Lilian looked up. Her eyes held pain. And something else.

I sat beside her. She didn't flinch. Just reached for my hand.

And I knew then she hadn't just kept me alive. She'd pulled me back from the edge. With her prayers. With her bruised hands and broken body and a faith that doesn't flinch when the devil's breathing down your neck.

From a darkness I couldn't walk out of on my own.

It took me years to understand what that meant. Decades, really.

But that day, in that room, with her leading prayer while I still smelled gunpowder—

She was the only thing standing between me and damnation.

Interlude - On The Porch

I LEAVE OUT the worst of it when I tell the story. The bruises. The blood. The way Lilian looked that day—like something sacred had been torn out of her. My grandkids don't need those images burned into their minds.

But I see it every time I tell it. All the violence and horror. And I relive the helplessness and rage all over again.

Tessa knows. She knows every dark detail. Every vile thing Caleb Mason ever did. And more than that, she knows what it cost me not to pull the trigger.

She's sitting beside me now, quiet, steady. Her hand rests on my arm, like it always does when the memories start to stir.

"That day," I say, voice low, "I learned the difference between vengeance and justice."

The kids lean in. Even the littlest one's gone still.

"I wanted blood. Thought if I killed Caleb, the world would balance out. But it wouldn't have. Would've just made me another man ruled by rage."

Tessa doesn't speak, but I feel her nod.

"Justice sets things right. Vengeance just wants someone to pay. And when you're hurting bad enough, you don't care which one you're chasing."

I glance at the oldest boy. He's watching me close, like he's trying to understand something bigger than the story.

"I spent years trying to help Flynn learn that. When it came to Galen." I pause. "But that's Flynn's story to tell."

I sit back, let the silence stretch as a gentle breeze moves across the porch.

"Bible says, 'Vengeance belongs to me; I will repay, says the Lord.' I didn't understand that back then. Not really. But Lilian did. She prayed when I couldn't. For my salvation. Even while I stood in a barn with murder in my heart."

I look out across the yard. The dusk light's fading. Coyotes'll be singing soon.

"She stood between me and damnation. And I didn't even know it."

I swallow down the bitter truth. Force my lips to speak it aloud.

"I taught them how to survive. How to fight. How to stay alive. But Lilian? She taught them something bigger. How to pray a man's soul toward salvation. Best lesson any of us ever learned."

I clear my throat. Shift in the rocker.

"After she healed, I got her to Prescott. That's where the next part begins. Keeping her safe. Keeping my sisters alive. Finally doing what I should've done years before."

I glance at the kids again. They're leaning in now.

"Flight to Prescott," I say. "That's what we called it."

And I know they'll remember that name.

Because it was the first time I started to believe we might actually make it.

8 - Flight to Prescott

———————

Fall 1892

FLYNN MET ME behind the barn, arms crossed, jaw tight.

"You sure about this?" he asked, voice low.

I nodded. "She's almost healed. Face looks better. She's got the dress near finished."

"She's still limping."

"She can walk. That's enough."

He looked past me toward the house. "You think Galen's watching?"

"I know he is."

Flynn rubbed the back of his neck. "Then why now?"

"Because if we wait any longer, who knows what Caleb will do. She needs to look respectable to get a safe job."

He didn't argue. Just stared at the horizon like he was trying to see trouble before it came.

"I need you to keep the others close," I said. "If Galen shows up, you act like we're in Congress. Buying feed. Nothing more."

Flynn nodded once. "You trust me with them?"

"I do."

He didn't speak for a moment. "I won't let him near them."

89

I clapped his shoulder. "I know."

Lilian's bruises had faded to yellow. She still winced when she bent too fast, but her eyes were clear again. She'd stitched the dress herself—soft blue cotton, neat seams, a collar that made her look like she belonged behind a desk, not in a ditch.

I'd brought her sewing jobs from town. Paid in coin and scraps of fabric. Justine and Hayley helped when they could, sneaking thread and needles from Galen's stores. Every stitch was a step toward freedom.

That morning, Lilian stood in the doorway, dress pressed, hair pinned up, and satchel packed.

She hugged each of them—Justine, Hayley, Flynn. Then she kneeled in front of Ike, cupped his face in her hands.

"I promise," she said. "I'll see you soon."

He nodded, eyes wide, trying not to cry. He was thirteen now. Same age I was when I lost Mama.

I helped Lilian into the wagon. She didn't look back.

The wagon groaned as we climbed. The trail narrowed, slick from last night's rain. One wrong turn and we'd be in the ravine. I kept the reins tight, jaw clenched, heart pounding with every bend.

Behind us, the ridgeline kicked up dust.

I didn't look back again. Didn't need to. I knew what that meant.

Galen.

Or one of his men.

I prayed Flynn would keep his wits. Say we were headed to Congress for feed. Maybe Galen wouldn't ask. Maybe he'd be too drunk to care.

But I didn't count on luck. Not anymore.

Lilian sat beside me, hands folded in her lap. She didn't speak. Didn't flinch. Just stared straight ahead like she'd already made peace with whatever came next.

She'd earned this escape. Every stitch of that dress, every hour bent over someone else's mending, every bruise she'd hidden with powder and prayer—it all led here.

I'd waited too long to get her out. Couldn't risk sending her into town with her face still swollen. No respectable job would take her like that. So we waited. And while we waited, she worked.

And now she was on her way to Prescott. To a find a job. To a house with a lock. To a life.

I wasn't sure we'd make it. But I knew we had to try.

By the time we reached Prescott, my nerves were frayed. The trail had tested every inch of me—switchbacks slick with rain.

Lilian didn't speak until we hit the edge of town.

"I can handle this, Shane. Just get me a room at the boardinghouse for a few nights. That's all I need."

"You sure?"

She nodded. "I've got the dress. I've got my name. I'll find work."

I wanted to argue. Wanted to stay. But I knew better. She needed space to stand on her own. Not a man hovering like she might break.

So I paid the landlady, helped her carry her satchel inside, and left before the sun dipped low enough to cast doubt.

I hated leaving her.

———

THREE WEEKS LATER, her letter came.

I recognized her handwriting before I opened it—tight, clean strokes, no wasted ink.

Shane,

I've taken a job at the Livestock Commission Office. Secretary work. The pay is steady, and the men are respectful. I've rented a small three-bedroom house near the square. It's modest, but safe. There's an opening at the dry goods store. A kind older gentleman owns it. He's holding the job for Justine. Please send her soon. We'll make room.

We'll make it work. I promise.
  Lilian

I set the letter down. Only a two-day window to get Justine there before the job was gone.

I made the decision.

Gave her our best horse. Told her to ride hard, sell it if she had to. Buy herself time. Buy herself safety.

Flynn didn't argue. Just helped her pack.

Hayley cried. Ike tried not to.

I watched Justine ride out, braid swinging behind her, satchel tied tight, eyes locked on the horizon.

Another sister safe.

But the cost was coming.

————

THE MONTHS TICKED by with Hayley ready to go at a moment's notice. Problem was Galen and his gang were planning something extensive. Something big.

They wouldn't leave. And they were using up our provisions fast.

We needed food, so I sent Flynn out to hunt and trap. He'd gotten better at. Still, he needed more practice.

Flynn came back empty-handed three days in a row.

I didn't blame him. The game was scarce; the weather turned cold earlier than usual. He was trying. That's all any of us could do.

But Hayley was ready. Had been ready for weeks. With her satchel packed, her escape dress sewn and hidden. All she needed was a horse and a clear shot at the trail.

I'd been waiting for Galen to leave again. For another opening.

It came on a gray morning in late November when Galen and most of his men rode out before dawn. Said they'd be gone four, maybe five days. Scouting, planning. I didn't ask what for. Never did.

"Today," I told Hayley after they'd been gone an hour. "Flynn, saddle the dappled mare. She's the strongest we've got left."

Flynn's eyes went wide. "We can't spare her, Shane. That's our best—"

"I know."

He understood then. We were gambling everything on this. The mare was worth money. Worth survival. But Hayley's safety was worth more.

Hayley stood in the kitchen doorway in her escape dress—simple brown calico, clean and pressed, a bonnet tied under her chin. She looked like any respectable young woman heading to town. Not a girl running for her life.

"You remember the directions?" I asked.

"I remember."

"You ride straight through. Don't stop except to water the horse. If anyone asks—"

"I'm visiting my aunt in Prescott. My sisters already live there." She said it smoothly, with no hesitation.

I nodded. Flynn brought the mare around. I helped Hayley mount, checked the satchel straps, and made sure the coin purse was secure in her pocket.

"Sell the mare when you get there," I said. "Use the money to help Lilian with rent until you find work."

"Shane—"

"Do it, Hayley. That's an order."

She nodded, jaw tight. Then she leaned down and kissed my cheek. "Thank you."

I stepped back. Flynn grabbed the reins one more time. "You be careful, you hear?"

"I will." She smiled at him, brave and bright. "Take care of Ike."

Then she kicked the mare into a trot and didn't look back.

We watched until she disappeared over the ridge. Then Flynn turned to me, shoulders sagging.

"We're in trouble now, aren't we?"

"Yeah," I said. "We are."

————

GALEN CAME BACK six days later.

I saw the dust first. Then the riders. More than had left. And behind them, a wagon creaked under the weight of crates and barrels.

My gut twisted.

They pulled into the yard just after sunset. Galen dismounted, stretched, and looked around like he owned the world.

"Where's Hayley?" he asked.

I'd prepared for this. Had my story ready. "Prescott. She's with Lilian and Justine now."

His face went still. "Is that so?"

"Yes, sir."

He stared at me. Long enough that sweat prickled down my back despite the cold. Then he smiled. It didn't reach his eyes.

"Well," he said. "Good for her."

He turned and walked toward the barn. The other men started unloading the wagon. Bart and two others I didn't recognize carried crates into the barn's hidden room. The padlock clicked shut behind them.

Flynn and I exchanged glances. Whatever they were planning, it was big. And we were stuck in the middle of it.

————

THEY STAYED FOR two months.

Ate through our winter stores like locusts. Drank our coffee, burned our wood, used our water. Galen said it was temporary. Said they'd be gone soon.

I believed him. Had to.

But watching Ike get thinner, watching Flynn's cheekbones sharpen, watching our supplies dwindle to nothing made me wonder if temporary would come too late.

I sent Flynn out to hunt every day. Some days he brought back a rabbit. Some days, a handful of quail. Once, a scraggly coyote that we boiled until the meat fell off the bones.

It wasn't enough.

By January, we were rationing what little remained. Giving Ike the largest portions. Pretended we weren't hungry, so he'd eat more.

Then one morning, I woke to smoke.

Not cook-fire smoke. Not the smell of breakfast or warmth or home.

Burning. Destruction. Loss.

I bolted from bed, ran outside in my undershirt and boots.

The barn was fine. The house was fine.

But the root cellar was on fire.

Our last food stores. The potatoes, the dried corn, the preserves—everything we'd been saving to stretch through spring—burning.

I ran toward it anyway. Stupid. Desperate. Flynn grabbed my arm.

"Shane, no! It's too far gone!"

He was right. The flames had already consumed the wooden door, the frame, everything. Black smoke poured into the gray dawn sky.

Behind us, Galen stood on the porch. Watching. Calm as Sunday morning.

"Shame about that fire," he said. "Must've been a spark from last night's cook fire. These old cellars, you know. Dangerous."

I turned toward him. Every muscle in my body coiled tight, ready to lunge, ready to—

Flynn's hand clamped down harder on my arm.

"Don't."

Galen smiled. "You boys should be more careful. Can't afford accidents like this when you're all alone out here."

Then he went back inside.

The fire burned for two hours. By the time it died, there was nothing left but ash and the smell of destruction.

That afternoon, Galen and his men loaded their wagon, saddled their horses, and rode out.

They took twelve head of cattle with them. The best of what remained. Left us with three malnourished cows, two sickly calves, and an ancient mule.

Flynn, Ike, and I stood in the yard and watched them go.

"Why?" Ike asked. His voice was small, confused. "Why would Pa do that?"

I didn't have an answer that wouldn't break him.

Flynn did. "Because the girls are safe now. And he can't stand that we got them out."

It was true. Every word.

Galen had punished us for winning.

That night, after Ike fell asleep, Flynn and I sat by the dying fire.

"We're not going to make it," he said.

"Yes, we are."

"Shane—"

"We are." I said it hard, like saying it strong enough would make it true. "The girls are safe. That's what matters. That was always the deal."

Flynn stared into the flames. "We agreed to that. All of us. I know."

"Then we stick to it."

He nodded. But neither of us believed we'd last until spring.

We'd saved our sisters.

Now we just had to survive the cost.

Interlude - By The Fire

───────────

WE MOVE BACK inside, and I light a fire. I can see the weight of the story settling on my grandchildren. Emma's eyes are wide, Jake's jaw is tight like he's trying not to cry.

"Grandpa," Emma says, "how did you make it?"

I look at Tessa. Her fingers curl around the armrest of her favorite chair, watching me with that expression that says she knows exactly what I'm thinking and exactly what I need to say.

"We almost didn't," I tell them honestly. "By February, we were down to one meal a day. Half-rations. Ike was so thin I could count every rib. Flynn stopped complaining about being hungry—that's when I knew it was bad."

"But you did make it," Jake insists. "You're here."

"God sent Deacon and Grady to save us," I say. The words still feel strange in my mouth after all these years, but they're true. I know that now.

Tessa reaches over and squeezes my hand. "What your grandfather didn't know then—what he couldn't see—was that God was already moving. While Shane, Flynn, and Ike were starving, the Lord was preparing their rescue."

"Lilian was working with Deacon Colter," I explain. "He was a livestock detective, investigating our father. She told him about us—about the boys left behind at the ranch. Deacon brought in Grady Thatcher, another detective I'd later partner with for years."

"Justine's husband," Tessa adds.

"Uncle Grady? He and Deacon came for you?" Emma asks.

"They came for us. Rode out to the ranch in March, just when we were at our lowest. If they'd waited another week..." I don't finish that sentence. Don't need to.

Tessa speaks up, her voice gentle but firm. "What your grandfather won't tell you is that God's timing was perfect. Not a day too early, not a day too late. The Lord preserved those three boys through the darkest winter of their lives, and then He sent exactly the right men at exactly the right moment."

"But we were starving," I protest, the way I always do when Tessa talks like this. "If God was protecting us, why'd He let it get that bad?"

She looks at me with patient love, the same look she's given me a thousand times over the years. "Because you had to reach the end of yourself, Shane. You had to learn that you couldn't do it all alone. That was the lesson. Not that God abandoned you, but that He was teaching you to receive help when it came."

The grandchildren are quiet, thinking about this.

"Your grandfather made an incredible sacrifice," Tessa continues, addressing them directly. "He sent all three of his sisters to safety even though it meant he and his brothers would suffer the consequences. That's the love Jesus talks about—laying down your life for your friends."

I tighten my jaw, trying to stem the rising emotion.

"We agreed to it," I say. "All three of us. Flynn, Ike, and me. We knew what would happen when Galen figured out all the girls were gone. We knew he'd punish us for it. But the girls were safe." I pause, throat tight. "That was all that mattered."

"And God honored that sacrifice," Tessa says softly. "He saw three boys choosing to suffer so their sisters could be free, and He sent rescue. Maybe not as fast as you wanted, but exactly when you needed it most."

Jake leans forward. "What happened when Grady and Deacon got there? Were you scared? Did you trust them?"

I almost laugh, remembering. "Son, by the time they showed up, I was too weak to be scared and too desperate to care about trust. They could've been outlaws for all I knew, and I still would've accepted their help. We needed food, and we needed out. That's all I understood."

"But they weren't outlaws," Emma says. "They were the good guys."

"They were," I confirm. "Deacon married Lilian eventually. Became my brother-in-law. Grady married Justine. Those two men changed the course of all our lives."

"God placed them in your path," Tessa adds. "And He gave them hearts that cared about justice and protecting the innocent. Your grandfather thinks it was luck or coincidence that brought them to the ranch that day. But I know better."

I shake my head, but there's no heat in it. We've had this conversation before. "Maybe you're right."

"I am right," she says, smiling. "But you're getting there. Slowly."

Emma climbs into my lap. She's almost too old for it, but not quite. "I'm glad they came for you, Grandpa. I'm glad you didn't die."

"Me too, sweetheart," I tell her, voice rough. "Me too."

"But Grandpa said he didn't believe in God then," Emma points out.

"He didn't," Tessa agrees. "But God believed in him. God saw a young man with a fierce heart and an unbreakable will, and He used that boy to protect five children through thirteen years of purgatory. Shane thought he was alone, carrying everything by himself. What he didn't know was that he was never alone. God gave him supernatural strength, wisdom beyond his years, and the endurance to keep going when any reasonable person would have given up."

I clear my throat, uncomfortable with the praise but knowing Tessa won't back down from this. She never does.

"Lilian prayed for us every day," I whisper. "After she got to Prescott, she prayed even harder. Prayed for rescue. For safety. For us to survive until help came." I pause. "Maybe Tessa's right. Maybe those prayers kept us alive."

"They did," Tessa says with absolute certainty. "Prayer moves mountains. It kept three starving boys breathing through the worst winter of their lives. It brought two detectives hundreds of miles to an isolated ranch at the exact right moment."

The room falls quiet except for the crackling of the dying fire.

"The next story," I tell my grandchildren, "is about that rescue. About the day Grady and Deacon rode into the yard and everything changed. I was twenty-six years old, and I was too weak to stand but still trying to protect my brothers."

"We want to hear it," Jake says immediately.

Emma nods against my chest. "We're ready, Grandpa."

Tessa stands, smoothing her skirt. "I'll make some cocoa first. This story needs cocoa."

As she heads to the kitchen, I gather my thoughts. The rescue. The moment everything shifted. The day I learned that sometimes—just sometimes—help really does come.

I just had to survive long enough to see it.

9 - The Last Morning

March 1893

I WOKE TO gray light and to the sound of Flynn coughing.

Not the rough, clear-your-throat kind. The wet, racking kind that comes from a body that's been pushed too far for too long.

I lay still on my bedroll, staring at the water-stained ceiling, and counted the days since Galen had left.

Four. Maybe five.

Time got slippery when you were this hungry.

Flynn coughed again. I turned my head and saw him curled on his side, knees drawn up, shaking under his threadbare blanket. Sixteen years old and thin as a fence post. I could see the sharp angles of his shoulders through his shirt.

Ike hadn't moved yet. That was good. The longer he slept, the less he'd feel the gnawing in his belly.

I pushed myself upright. My head swam for a moment, black spots dancing at the edges of my vision. I waited for it to pass, then stood.

The house was silent except for the wind rattling the loose boards on the north wall. Needed fixing. Had needed fixing for months. But you can't fix a house when you're trying to keep your brothers from starving.

I walked to the kitchen on legs that felt like they belonged to someone else. Opened the cupboards even though I knew what I'd find.

Nothing.

Checked the pantry anyway. Same result. Mouse droppings and dust.

I closed the door and leaned my forehead against it.

Four days. Maybe five.

The cattle were gone. The chickens were gone. Even the scrawny rooster that used to wake us at dawn had disappeared. Probably into someone's stew pot before Galen rode out.

We had three sickly cows left in the north pasture, too weak to be worth stealing. And one ancient mule that would die before summer came.

I'd gone hunting yesterday. Walked five miles before my legs gave out. Saw nothing but a hawk circling overhead, probably wondering if I'd keel over and save it the trouble of finding breakfast.

Flynn coughed again, harder this time.

I turned and looked at my brothers. Flynn's face was gray in the morning light, cheekbones standing out like knife blades. Ike was so small under his blanket I could barely see him.

Fourteen years old and starving.

Both of them starving.

And me? I was supposed to fix this. Supposed to keep them alive. That's what I'd done for thirteen years—kept all of us alive despite Galen, despite the hunger, despite everything. But I'd run out of options. Run out of tricks.

Run out of time.

I walked to the window and stared out at the dead land. March in the Arizona Territory. Too early for game to be plentiful. Too late for winter stores to last. The worst possible time to be abandoned.

Galen knew that when he left.

Behind me, I heard Flynn stir. "Shane?"

I turned. He'd pushed himself up on one elbow, his face pale and drawn.

"I was thinking," he said, his voice rough. "That cow in the north pasture. The one that's barely standing. We could—"

"No." I shook my head. "If we butcher her now, we'll have meat for a week. Maybe two. Then what? We need her alive. Need the chance she might recover, might breed, might give us something to build on when..." I trailed off.

When what? When Galen came back? When spring came? When help arrived?

None of those things were coming.

Flynn lay back down. "Yeah. You're right."

But I wasn't sure I was. Wasn't sure about anything anymore except that my brothers were dying, and I couldn't stop it.

I walked outside. The morning air was chilly, biting through my shirt. I should've grabbed a coat, but I didn't have the energy to go back for it.

The barn stood open, its door hanging crooked on broken hinges. I walked inside, more out of habit than purpose. Checked the stalls even though I knew they were empty. Looked at the tack even though we had nothing left to saddle.

Then I saw it. The hidden room where Galen kept his records. The door hung open. He'd left in a hurry, hadn't bothered to lock it.

I stepped inside.

Papers covered a makeshift desk. Names, dates, brands. A complete record of every crime Galen Harper and his gang had committed over the past five years. Rustling operations. Fencing schemes. Payoffs to corrupt officials.

Evidence. Enough to hang him and half his crew.

For just a moment, I let myself imagine it. Turning this over to the law. Watching Galen arrested, tried, and convicted. Watching him pay for every bruise, every threat, every hungry night he'd caused.

But who would I give it to? The sheriff was in Galen's pocket. The nearest honest lawman was two days' ride, and I didn't have the strength to make it there, much less back.

I left the papers where they were and walked back to the house.

Flynn was up now, trying to get Ike to wake up. But Ike just mumbled something and rolled over, too weak to even sit up.

"Shane." Flynn's voice cracked. "What do we do?"

I looked at my brothers. At the house that had been our prison for thirteen years. At the empty cupboards and the desperate situation and the complete absence of any way forward.

"I don't know," I said.

It was the first time I'd admitted that out loud.

Flynn stared at me. "What do you mean you don't know? You always know. You always have a plan."

"Not this time."

"But—"

"I don't know!" The words came out harsher than I meant. "I don't know what to do, Flynn. I've got nothing left. No food, no money, no options. I can't fix this."

The silence that followed hurt worse than hunger.

Then Ike spoke from his bedroll, his voice barely a whisper. "Then maybe we should pray."

Flynn and I both turned to stare at him.

"Lilian always said God answers prayers," Ike continued. "Maybe... maybe we should try."

I wanted to tell him that God didn't answer prayers. That if He did, we wouldn't be in this mess. That we'd been abandoned by everyone, including whatever deity Lilian believed in.

But I didn't have the heart to crush whatever hope Ike was clinging to.

"You pray if you want," I mumbled. "Can't hurt."

Ike closed his eyes. His lips moved, but I couldn't hear the words.

I walked back outside. Couldn't stand to watch my youngest brother pray to a God who'd never once shown up for us.

That's when I saw the dust.

Two riders, coming up the road at an easy pace.

My hand went to my hip, but I'd pawned my revolver two months ago for flour that was long gone.

"Flynn," I called. "We've got company."

He appeared in the doorway, squinting against the morning sun. "Who is it?"

"Don't know yet."

The riders drew closer. Both young men, maybe early twenties. The one on the left was dark-haired with sharp eyes that missed nothing. The one on the right sat his horse with the confidence of a man who'd seen trouble and knew how to handle it.

Not Galen's gang. These men sat their horses different. Professional. Confident.

Lawmen, maybe.

Or trouble.

At this point, I wasn't sure there was a difference.

"Stay inside," I told Flynn. "Keep Ike quiet."

"What are you going to do?"

"Talk to them."

I walked into the yard, positioning myself between the house and the riders. Unarmed. Exhausted. Barely able to stand.

But I'd be hanged before I let anyone past me to get to my brothers.

"Shane Harper?" the one with the commanding bearing asked.

I nodded.

"My name's Grady Thatcher. This is Deacon Colter. Your sister Lilian sent us."

The world tilted sideways.

Lilian.

I must've swayed, because Deacon dismounted quickly

and caught my arm.

"Easy," he said. "When's the last time you ate?"

I shook my head. I couldn't remember.

"Your father here?" Grady asked, scanning the property with the practiced eye of a man who knew how to assess threats.

"No. He left. Three, four days ago. Maybe five."

"And your brothers?"

"Inside."

Grady and Deacon exchanged a quick, grim look. They'd expected bad, but this was worse.

"Let's get you boys out of here," Grady said. "Lilian's got food waiting. And beds. And safety."

I stared at him. Tried to make sense of the words.

Rescue.

After thirteen years of fighting alone, after months of watching my brothers waste away, after all the impossible choices and crushing weight—

Help had come.

"All of us?" My voice cracked on the words. "All three?"

"All three," Deacon confirmed. His grip on my arm steadied. "You're safe now, Shane. All of you."

I tried to answer. Couldn't.

Something broke loose in my chest. Something I'd been holding in place through sheer force of will for longer than I could remember.

I turned my head away so they wouldn't see my face.

"Hey." Grady's voice was gentle. "It's over. You did it. You kept them alive."

I nodded, not trusting myself to speak.

Behind me, I heard the door open. Flynn's voice, tentative and disbelieving. "Shane? What's happening?"

I wiped my face with the back of my hand and turned around.

"Pack your things," I told him. My voice steadied. "We're leaving."

"Leaving where?"

"Prescott. To see the girls."

Flynn's eyes went wide. "All of us?"

"All of us."

For the first time in months—years—I watched hope light up my brother's face.

And I finally let myself believe it.

We'd made it.

Against all odds, despite every obstacle, through all the hunger and fear and impossible choices…

We'd survived.

Interlude - By The Fire

———————

THE FIRE HAS burned down to coals. Emma's still in my lap, her breathing steady and calm despite the heaviness of the story. Jake sits straighter than before, like he's aged a year just listening.

"What happened next, Grandpa?" Emma asks quietly. "After they took you to Prescott?"

I look at Tessa. She sets down her knitting and gives me that gentle nod that says go ahead, tell them the rest.

"We went to Prescott," I say. "To the house where Lilian, Justine, and Hayley were living. We could see it from the hill—every window blazing with light. Like a beacon."

"Were they happy to see you?" Jake asks.

"They rushed out before we'd even dismounted. Lilian was crying and laughing at the same time. Justine hugged Flynn so hard she lifted him off her feet, even though he was half a foot taller than her. Hayley wouldn't let go of me."

My throat tightens at the memory. "First time in months I'd seen my sisters. First time we'd all been together and safe at the same time."

"And then what?" Emma prompts.

"Then we healed. Took weeks before Flynn and Ike could walk without getting winded. Months before we stopped flinching at every sound. We ate real meals. And pie. Justine baked us pies. Slept in real beds. Learned what it felt like to wake up without fear."

"And Galen?" Jake's voice hardens on the name. "Your father?"

"Grady and Deacon tracked him down. Arrested him and his entire gang. Galen went to Yuma Prison for fifteen years. The worst of them were hanged or imprisoned. Justice was served."

"Good," Jake says fiercely.

"It was good," I agree. "But more than that, we were free. For the first time in thirteen years, we didn't have to look over our shoulders. We could just... live."

Tessa speaks up then, her voice warm. "And they didn't just survive, children. They thrived. Every single Harper sibling took what they'd been through and used it to protect others. They chose justice over vengeance. Protection over profit. They chose to fight for others the way they'd wished someone had fought for them."

"There's one more story," Tessa says gently. "One more piece your grandfather needs to tell you about those early years."

I nod. She's right.

"Five years after our rescue—January 1, 1898—the four of us who'd survived together went back to the Harper Ranch. Me, Flynn, Hayley, and Ike. Lilian and Justine stayed in Prescott because they'd moved on, built new lives. But the four of us needed closure."

"What did you do?" Jake asks.

"We burned it down," I say simply. "The house. The barn. All of it. We stood there and watched thirteen years of suffering go up in smoke."

Emma's eyes are wide. "The whole ranch?"

"The whole ranch. It needed to die so we could truly live."

The room falls quiet. The fire crackles. Outside, the night is peaceful and safe.

"That last story," I tell my grandchildren, "is about endings and beginnings. About letting go of the past so you can build a future. About watching everything that hurt us turn to ash, and deciding what we'd build from those ashes."

"We want to hear it," Jake says immediately.

Emma nods against my chest. "Please, Grandpa."

I look at Tessa. She smiles and stands. "I'll make more cocoa. This story deserves cocoa."

As she heads to the kitchen, I gather my thoughts. The burning. The oath. The moment everything changed from survival to purpose.

The moment my first family truly became whole.

10 - Ashes and Oaths

January 1, 1898

I STOOD AT the edge of what used to be our home and tried to remember if I'd ever felt anything good here.

The ranch house sagged like a dying animal. The barn roof had caved in on the north side. Tumbleweeds piled against the corral fence where we used to keep the horses— back when we had horses worth keeping. The well still stood, its wooden frame weathered gray.

Four and a half years since Grady and Deacon pulled Flynn, Ike, and me out of this place. Four and a half years, and the memories still had teeth.

"Well?" Hayley's voice cut through my thoughts. She stood with her hands on her hips, that familiar stubborn set to her jaw. "Are we doing this or not?"

Flynn grinned, wild and reckless as ever. "I say we burn it to the ground."

Ike shifted his weight, nervous. The youngest of us, barely eighteen now, was still trying to find his place among siblings who'd been forged in fire long before he could re-member. "I don't know. Lilian—"

"Isn't here," Hayley interrupted. "And if she were, she'd understand."

I wasn't sure about that. Lilian had made her peace with

this place years ago, found her healing through faith and family. But Lilian had escaped early. She hadn't stayed to watch it all crumble. Hadn't made the choices I'd made to keep the rest of them alive.

"Shane?" Hayley looked at me, waiting.

I pulled a toothpick from my pocket and stuck it between my teeth. Thinking. Always thinking, always calculating, even now when the war was long over.

"It's our land," I said finally. "Territory gave it back to us. No law against burning down our own property."

"Technically—" Ike started.

"Technically, nothing." I met his eyes. "This place needs to die. Should've burned it down years ago."

Hayley produced a box of matches from her coat pocket. Ike immediately tried to snatch them away.

"Hayley! You're insane!"

She danced back, too quick for him. Always had been. "It's not like I didn't tell you my plan before we came here."

"Lilian would not approve."

Flynn laughed, a sharp bark that meant he was enjoying himself. "I'm not sure Hay cares."

She didn't. I could see it in her eyes—that same fierce determination that had kept her alive when Victor Mason cornered her in the barn all those years ago. My little sister, who'd learned to be dangerous because I'd taught her she had to be.

"Are we gonna do this or not?" The words came out rougher than I meant them.

Ike held the matches high, out of Hayley's reach. She glared at him, then turned that glare on Flynn. Something passed between them—that almost twin-like connection they'd always had, reading each other without words. Honed through their sparring matches.

Flynn swiped the matches back from Ike and tossed them to Hayley.

"Just don't burn down the entire valley," he said, grinning.

I watched Hayley strike the first match. The sulfur smell hit my nose, sharp and acrid. She dropped it onto the line of kerosene we'd poured around the house earlier.

The flames caught. Spread. Raced along the fuel line like they'd been waiting years for this moment.

Maybe they had.

The south wall went up first.

I stared at those weathered boards and remembered the Christmas I was thirteen. One rabbit for six kids. I'd stood in that kitchen and portioned out meat so small you could barely call it a meal, trying to make sure everyone got something.

Lilian had smiled at me as if I'd brought a feast for a king. "You did good, Shane."

I hadn't done good. I'd barely done enough.

The flames climbed higher, eating through the wood with a hungry crackle.

Flynn stood beside me, his face lit orange by the growing fire. "Feels good, doesn't it?"

"Yeah." My voice sounded hollow even to my own ears. "Yeah, it does."

But it didn't. Not exactly. Watching it burn felt necessary, like lancing a wound. But good? I wasn't sure I remembered what good felt like anymore.

The fire reached the kitchen window. Glass shattered from the heat. I flinched.

Behind that window, I'd stood watch so many nights. Counting heads. Making sure everyone was accounted for. Watching for riders on the horizon—Galen's gang coming back, bringing violence and fear with them.

The red bandanna system. That had been brilliant, if I said so myself. Simple. Effective. Kept my sisters safe when I couldn't be everywhere at once.

Except it hadn't kept them safe. Not really. Not from everything.

Hayley moved closer to the fire, her face set in hard lines. She was twenty-one now, a Pinkerton agent, dangerous and competent and so much stronger than she should've had to be.

"You alright?" I asked her.

She nodded without looking at me. "Just making sure it burns properly."

The barn was next. The entire structure groaned as flames caught the old wood. I remembered the hidden room where Galen's gang used to hole up. The whistle system— one short blast meant all-clear, two blasts meant trouble.

I'd memorized those signals. Used them. Survived by them.

Now they burned.

"Shane," Ike said. He'd moved up beside me, his youthful face troubled. "Do you think... do you think we're doing the right thing?"

"There is no right or wrong here." I flicked my toothpick toward the fire, watched it disappear into the flames. "There's just what we need to survive. Same as it's always been."

"But we're not just surviving anymore. We're—"

"We're getting rid of a corpse," Flynn interrupted. "This place died a long time ago. We're just burying it proper."

Flynn had always been the blunt one. Called things what they were. Maybe that's why he and Hayley got along so well—neither of them had patience for pretending things were better than they were.

I watched him watching the fire, saw the satisfaction in his eyes, the grim pleasure. Flynn had wanted to kill Galen. Might still do it if he got the chance. That rage had never quite left him, even after we got out.

I'd put that rage there. Taught him to fight, to survive, to be hard enough to make it through. Turned my little brother into a weapon because the alternative was watching him break.

At least Ike had the best hope of a normal life. Not that he was without his scars.

The fire roared now, fully engaged. Heat rolled over us in waves. Smoke thickened the air, an eye-watering reminder of the purgatory we had escaped. I took a step back, purely instinctual, checking that my family was at a safe distance.

Still protecting them. Still calculating. Couldn't seem to stop, even when the threat was one we'd created ourselves.

As the flames died down to a steady burn, we stood in silence. Watching years of pain turn to ash.

Hayley let out a long sigh, her shoulders dropping. "It's really gone."

"Good riddance," Flynn muttered.

Ike just stared at the fire, his expression unreadable.

I felt... empty. Like I'd been carrying something heavy for so long that now that I'd set it down, I didn't know what to do with my hands.

"Shane?" Hayley's voice was soft. Worried. "You okay?"

Was I? I'd spent half my life keeping them alive in that house. Thirteen years old to twenty-six. The most formative years of a man's life, spent in a war zone. And now it was just... gone. Smoke and ash and memory.

"I'm fine," I said.

None of them believed me. I could see it in their faces. But they didn't push. They knew better.

The sun dropped toward the horizon, painting the smoke orange and red and gold. Beautiful, in a terrible sort of way.

Flynn started setting up the tent. "I'll take first watch."

"No," Hayley said. "I will."

"You sure?" Ike asked.

"Yes."

We went through the motions—setting camp, preparing for the night. Normal things. Family things. The kind of things families did when they weren't constantly bracing for violence.

Before we turned in, I did something unexpected.

I reached out and clasped Ike's hand. Then Hayley's. They looked at me, surprised, then instinctively completed the circle with Flynn.

"There's something I want to say," I said.

The words felt strange in my mouth. I wasn't the one who made speeches. That was Ike's territory, or Lilian's. But this... this felt right. Necessary.

Years ago, when Lilian still lived at home, she'd read aloud from the Bible one Sunday morning. Most of it washed over me—I'd stopped listening to talk about God saving people when it was clear He wasn't saving us. But one verse stuck. Dug in deep and wouldn't let go.

I'd memorized it. Turned it over in my mind during the darkest times. Held onto it like a drowning man grips driftwood.

"When justice is executed," I said, my voice rougher than I intended, "it is a joy to the righteous but a terror to evildoers." I paused. "Proverbs 21:15."

Flynn's grip tightened on my hand. Hayley's eyes widened slightly—she'd never heard me quote Scripture before.

"Justice executed," Flynn repeated. "I like that."

"It's what we do," Hayley said. "What we've always done, in our own way."

They all looked at me. Waiting.

I thought about the choices I'd made. The lines I'd crossed. The things I'd done to keep them alive—things that haunted me in the quiet hours, things I'd never tell them about, never burden them with.

Was that justice? Or just survival?

"Justice," I said finally, testing the word. It felt foreign in my mouth, too clean for hands as dirty as mine. But maybe that was the point. Maybe that's what we needed it to be now—something clean, something to aim for. "Yeah. Justice."

"We dedicate our lives to it," Ike continued, his eyes bright with conviction. "Against men like our father. Against evil that preys on the innocent."

Flynn nodded fiercely. Hayley's jaw set with determination.

And I... I thought about Galen. About the Mason brothers. About every criminal I'd helped Grady hunt down over the past four years as a Livestock Detective. Every rustler we'd caught, every operation we'd dismantled.

Maybe that was justice. Maybe that's what happened when you stopped running and started fighting back.

"Against evil," I repeated. Not a question. A statement. An oath.

We stood there, four siblings bound by blood, by affliction, and by something greater still—the resolve to redeem what was lost and kindle hope from the embers.

When we finally broke apart and headed for our bedrolls, I stayed outside a few minutes longer. Watching the embers glow in the darkness. Watching the last pieces of our childhood home collapse into itself.

Hayley had been right. We needed this. Needed to watch it burn, needed to stand together and choose what came next.

Tomorrow, we'd douse the ashes. Head to Congress and catch the train. I'd start work with Burt Mossman at the Aztec Land & Cattle Company, alongside Flynn and Hayley. Three Harper siblings going undercover to root out rustlers.

Justice executed.

I pulled out another toothpick, stuck it between my teeth, and smiled into the darkness. Not much of a smile—I was out of practice—but it was there.

The war was over. We'd survived.

Now we'd do something with that survival. Turn it into purpose. Into justice.

The old Harper Ranch was dead. Let it stay dead.

We were building something new now. Something better.

And for the first time in longer than I could remember, I believed it might actually be possible.

————

THE FIRE HAD burned down to coals by the time I finally turned in. Flynn was already snoring softly in the tent. Ike mumbled something in his sleep—probably arguing a case even in his dreams. Hayley kept watch, sitting cross-legged by the dying fire, her rifle across her lap.

Always vigilant. I'd taught her that.

"Get some sleep, Hay," I said.

She looked up at me, and in the firelight, I could see the little girl she'd been—arranging pebbles by the well, innocent and unaware of the danger circling her.

Then I blinked, and she was twenty-one again. Hard and competent and alive.

"In a bit," she said. "I want to make sure it's really out."

I understood. We all needed our own ways of making sure it was really over.

I crawled into the tent, lay on my bedroll, and stared at the canvas above me.

In the morning, we'd leave this place for the last time. Leave it burned and buried and done.

In the morning, we'd start the next chapter.

But tonight, I let myself remember. Let myself feel the weight of everything it had taken to get here. Let myself grieve for the boy I'd been at thirteen, before I learned what it cost to keep people alive.

Tomorrow, we'd pursue justice.

Tonight, I'd let the ashes settle.

And somewhere in the darkness, I thought I heard Lilian's voice from all those years ago: "You did good, Shane."

Maybe I had. Maybe keeping them alive had been enough.

Maybe it was time to believe that.

The last thing I saw before sleep took me was the faint orange glow through the tent fabric. The last embers of our past, finally burning out.

Good riddance.

And good morning to whatever came next.

Closing - By The Fire

THE FIRE IN the hearth has burned down to glowing embers, casting long shadows across the room. Emma's fallen asleep in my lap, her breathing soft and steady. Jake sits on the floor at my feet, chin resting on his knees, eyes distant like he's seeing something far away.

"Grandpa," he says, "that verse you quoted. The one about justice. That's the Harper family motto, isn't it?"

"It is."

"Tell us what it means," he says. "Really means. Not just the words."

I look at Tessa. She's set aside her knitting completely now, watching me with those patient eyes that have seen me through so many hard conversations.

"Proverbs 21:15," I begin. "When justice is executed, it is a joy to the righteous but a terror to evildoers." I pause, choosing my words carefully. "That night at the burning ranch, I quoted it for the first time out loud. Lilian used to read Scripture to us when we were kids, and that one verse... it stuck. Like a hook in my mind that wouldn't let go."

"Even though you didn't believe?" Jake asks.

"Even though I didn't believe. I held onto it like a drowning man grips driftwood—didn't know why, didn't trust where it came from, but knew I needed something to keep my head above water."

Tessa speaks up, her voice gentle. "Your grandfather was holding onto truth even when he didn't recognize it as truth. God's Word has power whether we believe in it or not."

"That night," I continue, "we made it our family oath. Right there in the firelight with our childhood burning behind us, we decided the Harper name would mean justice. Real justice. Not revenge. Not violence for its own sake. Justice that protects the innocent and terrifies the wicked."

"And you all kept that oath," Jake says.

"We did. Every one of us chose careers that let us pursue justice. Lilian and Justine supported us, prayed for us, reminded us why we fought. Hayley tracked down criminals through investigation and sharp thinking. Flynn hunted down the worst of the worst as a U.S. Marshal. Ike prosecuted them in court, made sure the law worked the way it should. And I..." I pause. "I wore a Ranger's badge and tried to make the territory safer."

"That verse—" Tessa begins, then stops. Looks at me. "May I?"

I nod.

"That verse isn't just about punishment," she tells Jake and Emma, who's stirring awake now. "It's about the proper order of things. When evil is dealt with—when justice is truly executed—good people can rest easy. They can raise families without fear. Plant crops without worrying about raids. Build lives that matter. But evildoers? They should be terrified. Because justice is coming."

Jake processes this. "So it's not about revenge."

"No," I say firmly. "Revenge is personal. It's about settling scores and satisfying your own anger. Justice is about protecting others. About making sure what happened to us doesn't happen to anyone else."

"Did you ever want revenge?" he asks. "Against your father?"

I think about Galen. About watching him get sentenced to Yuma Prison. About the rage that used to consume me when I was younger.

"I did," I admit. "For years, I wanted him dead. Wanted to be the one to do it. But you know what I learned? Revenge wouldn't have brought my mother back. Wouldn't have given us those thirteen years of childhood. Wouldn't have healed a single scar."

"What did heal them?" Emma asks sleepily.

"Time," I tell her. "Family. Purpose. And—" I glance at Tessa, who's smiling—"learning that I didn't have to carry everything alone."

"And faith," Tessa adds quietly. "Don't forget faith, Shane."

"And faith," I concede. "Though that part took me longer than most."

The room falls quiet. Outside, I can hear the night sounds—crickets, a distant coyote, and the wind in the trees. Peaceful sounds. Safe sounds.

"I tell you these stories," I say, gathering my thoughts for what I need them to understand, "not to make you sad or scared. I tell you so you know what you come from. So you understand that the Harper name means something."

"It means you don't abandon family," Jake says, remembering.

"It means you fight for what's right, even when it costs you," Emma adds.

"It means you protect those who can't protect themselves," I finish. "And it means you pursue justice—not revenge, not violence, but real justice that makes the world safer for good people."

Jake stands up, something resolved in his face. "I want to remember that verse, Grandpa. Proverbs 21:15. I want to make it mean something in my life too."

Something loosens in my chest. Something I didn't know was still tight.

"You already do, son," I tell him. "Just by being kind to others. By standing up for what's right on the schoolyard. By choosing courage when it would be easier to look away. Justice isn't always about badges and guns. Sometimes it's about choosing to do right when no one's watching."

"But it always matters," Tessa adds. "Whether you're a Ranger chasing outlaws or a child standing up for a friend being bullied. Justice executed is joy for the righteous."

Emma yawns against my chest. "I'm glad the bad ranch burned down, Grandpa. I'm glad you got to start over."

"Me too, sweetheart."

"And I'm glad you met Grandma."

Tessa laughs softly. "I'm glad of that too."

I look around at my comfortable home. At my wife who's taught me that strength can be gentle. At my grandchildren who'll never know the fear I lived with daily. At the life we've built from ashes and oaths.

"You know what the best part is?" I tell them. "You don't have to fight the way we did. You don't have to survive the way we survived. Your great-aunts and great-uncles and I—we paid that price so you wouldn't have to."

"But you still have to choose justice," Tessa says firmly. "That part doesn't change. Every generation has to decide what they'll stand for."

"What will you stand for?" I ask my grandchildren.

Jake doesn't hesitate. "Justice. Protection. Family. The Harper way."

Emma nods sleepily. "What Grandpa said. Terror to evildoers, joy to... the good people."

"The righteous," I correct gently. "Joy to the righteous."

"That's us, right?" she asks.

"That's us," I confirm.

Tessa stands, smoothing her skirt. "Time for bed, children. Your grandfather's told you enough stories for one night. And your parents are picking you up early."

As she leads them toward their rooms, Jake turns back. "Grandpa? Thank you. For keeping your first family alive. For making the Harper name mean something good."

"You're welcome, son."

After they're gone, I sit by the dying fire and think about

that night five years after our rescue. Four siblings standing in the firelight, making an oath we didn't fully understand. Choosing justice when we could have chosen revenge. Choosing purpose when we could have stayed broken.

We kept that oath. All of us.

Tessa comes back, sits on the arm of my chair. Her hand finds mine.

"You did good, Shane," she says quietly.

The words hit me harder than they should. That's what Lilian said to me on Christmas Eve, 1880. After I'd brought home one skinny rabbit and tried to feed six hungry kids.

"Did I?" I ask.

"You kept them alive. You turned suffering into purpose. You built a legacy worth passing down." She squeezes my hand. "You did good."

I pull her closer, rest my head against her side.

Outside, the night is peaceful. Inside, my family sleeps safe and warm.

In the morning, my grandchildren will wake up without fear. They'll eat breakfast without worrying if there'll be lunch. They'll play without calculating escape routes.

That's what it was all for.

That's what made every impossible choice, every sacrifice, every scar worth bearing.

I kept my first family alive.

I built my second family with love.

And this third generation? They get to simply live.

Justice executed.

Joy to the righteous.

The Harper way.

Author's Note

———

WHEN I SAT down to write *The Traitor's Badge*, I needed to understand Shane Harper as the man he'd become at thirty-seven. To do that, I had to go back to the beginning.

What started as a simple character exercise turned into something much bigger. A series of short stories emerged, each one peeling back another layer of Shane's past. To truly grasp who he was as a man, I first had to understand what it meant to be born Galen Harper's oldest son. And all the impossible burdens that came with that inheritance.

As I wrote these stories, I found myself returning to a deleted scene I'd originally drafted for *The Rustler Hunter*. That scene—the burning of the old Harper ranch—was the Harper's refining fire and the birth of their oath. I'd written it in Hayley's perspective, but it never quite fit that story. Now, years later, I realized why. It wasn't Hayley's moment.

It was Shane's.

I reworked that scene from his point of view, and suddenly everything clicked. From the first word I wrote in the prequel *Blood Justice*, I knew Shane's siblings saw him as their true father—especially the three youngest: Hayley, Flynn, and Ike. That truth shaped every decision Shane made, every sacrifice he endured.

As I wrote, certain questions kept surfacing: What would make a man become the opposite of his outlaw father? What about Shane made him stay to protect his siblings when he really could have walked away? What did it cost him to become the man who raised them?

All these questions converged within these pages. What began as disconnected short stories suddenly felt like a unified narrative. The interludes between scenes wove everything together—Shane's voice reflecting on those brutal years from the safety and distance of his later life, surrounded by the family he built and the legacy he chose.

The novella became something I hadn't planned but desperately needed to write: a complete portrait of how a terrified thirteen-year-old boy became the steady, capable man who would later earn the name Arizona Ranger Shane Harper.

I hope you enjoyed this glimpse into the Harper siblings' origins—into the ashes they rose from and the oaths they made to each other. Understanding Shane's past makes his story in *The Traitor's Badge* (Harper's Justice Book 3) all the richer.

I'll see you within the pages of *The Rustler Hunter*, where the Harper siblings' journey toward justice begins.

Ride tall, friend.

R.J. Sloane

About the Author

R.J. SLOANE CAPTURES the raw spirit of the American frontier in action-packed westerns that don't shy away from the harsh realities of territorial justice. Drawing inspiration from modern classics like *Longmire*, *Yellowstone*, and *Murdoch Mysteries*, R.J.'s stories blend historical authenticity with the timeless struggle between law and lawlessness.

A passionate student of Southwest history, R.J. spends countless hours researching the legendary lawmen of the region—from the Arizona Rangers to the territorial marshals who tamed pivotal frontier towns like Phoenix, Tombstone, Prescott, and beyond. Growing up watching John Wayne, James Garner, and Clint Eastwood westerns with dad on lazy Sunday afternoons instilled a deep appreciation for authentic frontier storytelling. This combination of classic western influence and dedicated historical research brings depth and authenticity to every story.

The Harper Justice series follows a family of territorial lawmen as they navigate the dangerous transition from frontier chaos to civilized order, where doing what's right often means defying what's legal.

Website: https://rjsloanewesterns.com
Facebook: rjsloane.westerns
X (twitter): @RJSloaneWest

Books by This Author

The Harper name once struck fear in honest folk across the Arizona Territory. Now it strikes terror in outlaws. The six children of notorious criminal Galen Harper have turned their family legacy inside out, becoming the very lawmen their father spent his life outrunning. As Pinkerton agents, federal marshals, and territorial rangers, they're hunting down men just like the one who raised them. In the untamed frontier of 1898–1904, justice has a new name: Harper.

Ashes and Oaths (Origins) – Young Shane Harper

Blood Justice (Prequel) – Grady Thatcher

The Rustler Hunter (Book 1) – Hayley Harper

The Maverick Marshal (Book 2) – Flynn Harper

The Traitor's Badge (Book 3) – Shane Harper

The Attorney's Vendetta (Book 4) – Ike Harper

START HARPER'S JUSTICE WITH

The Rustler Hunter by R.J. Sloane

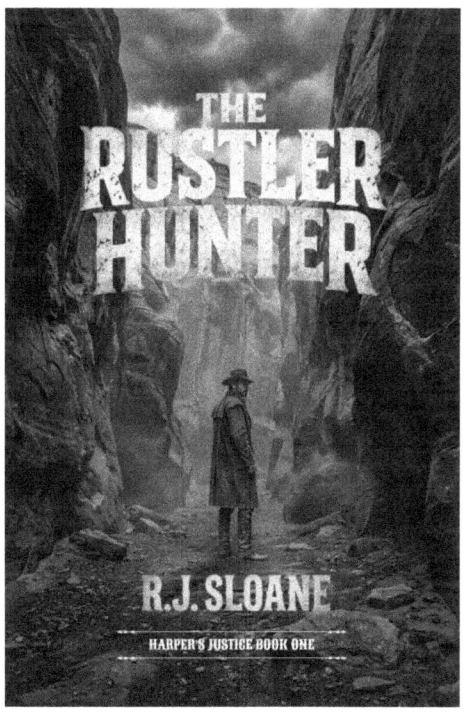

When forty-one successful manhunts make you a legend, there's only one way left to go—down.

J.J. Westin, the infamous Rustler Hunter, goes undercover at Arizona Territory's largest cattle ranch to expose the rustlers bleeding it dry. The thieves aren't just stealing cattle. They're trusted cowboys operating from inside the bunkhouse.

What he doesn't expect is Hayley Harper, the tough-as-nails cook with secrets of her own. She's a Pinkerton agent working the same case and the daughter of notorious outlaw Galen Harper.

When their covers are blown, they uncover something far deadlier than rustling. A corruption network spanning three territories. With enemies closing in and bullets flying, the legendary manhunter and the outlaw's daughter must survive the badlands of 1898 Arizona, where trust is deadly and justice comes at gunpoint.

In the shadow of Canyon Diablo, where the historic Aztec Land & Cattle Company's Hashknife outfit controlled over a million acres of the Arizona Territory's most lawless land.

Desert Life Media

There Is Life in The Desert

Entertainment-first Christian fiction set in the Southwest, featuring redemption, family, and faith

Publishing clean, wholesome, and uplifting fiction since 2010

---

desertlifemedia.com